PRAIRIE SCHOONER
BOOK PRIZE IN FICTION

Editor: Kwame Dawes

Domesticated Wild Things

and Other Stories

Xhenet Aliu

University of Nebraska Press / Lincoln and London

Library of Congress
Cataloging-in-Publication Data
Aliu, Xhenet, 1978–
[Short stories. Selections]
Domesticated wild things, and
other stories / Xhenet Aliu.
p. cm. — (Prairie Schooner
Book Prize in Fiction)
ISBN 978-0-8032-7183-8
(pbk.: alk. paper)
I. Title.
PS3601.L3967D66   2013
813'.6—dc23   2013006404

Set in Lyon by Laura Wellington.
Designed by Nathan Putens.

For Capt. Michael Jon Pelkey

Contents

ix   Acknowledgments

1   You Say Tomato

19   The Kill Jar

37   Ramon Beats the Crap Out of George, a Man Half His Size

49   Mandatory Evacuations

51   Flipping Property

65   Nadja Rides the Bear

81   Feather Ann

97   Two Assholes

111   Two-Step Snake

123   How to Play Shit

125   Domesticated Wild Things

Acknowledgments

These stories would not have been born without the nurturing of many incredibly generous mentors, advocates, and friends, including, in sloppy chronological order: the faculty and *Folio* crew at Southern Connecticut State University, especially Tim Parrish and Jason Labbe; the creative writing department at the University of North Carolina at Wilmington, notably Robert Anthony Siegel, Philip Gerard, Wendy Brenner, and Rebecca Lee, as well as my MFA peers; the Bread Loaf Writers' Conference, with a special shout-out to the waiter group of 2008, the social staffs of 2009–11, and big bosses Ru Freeman, Eugene Cross, and Matthew Olzmann; my sisters in fiction Gwendolyn Knapp, Jennine Capó Crucet, and Patricia Engel; all-around inspirers Christopher Rhodes and Latoya Jones; my adoptive creative writers at the University of Utah; the Elizabeth George Foundation; and about a thousand more. Thanks and my heart to Timothy O'Keefe for never wavering and for usually taking care of the dinner dishes.

Much gratitude to the following publications for having previously provided a home for some of the stories in this collection: "Flipping Property" in the *Barcelona Review*, "You Say Tomato" in *Glimmer Train*, and "How to Play Shit" and "Mandatory Evacuations" in *Hobart*. Thanks to my agent extraordinaire Julie Barer and to the writers Jim Shepard, Randall Kenan, Sigrid Nunez, Stacy

D'Erasmo, Kwame Dawes, Sherman Alexie, Colin Channer, and to the staff at *Prairie Schooner* and the University of Nebraska Press.

Mad love and gratitude to Mama and Chuck; my brother, Kyjtim; my brother from another mother, Michael; and my sisters from another mister, Sarah, Kimberly, and Kristen; and to the rest of the Misavage and Pelkey clans. Thank you for showing me how to work to exhaustion, take a punch, land a punch, and love like crazy.

Thanks to the Aliu and Poshka families across the United States, Strugë, Tiranë, and everywhere else you've landed for letting me know you haven't forgotten. To my late father, Petrit: in the end it was a gift.

DOMESTICATED WILD THINGS,

AND OTHER STORIES

You Say Tomato

My mother ate taycos and tortillia chips. She had good idears. She said that Mac was playing Nytendo, that he needed some deroderizer for his pits, that my real father had told her his name meant *warrior* in Albanian but it was actually more like Shit For Brains. My father was a Moslem, which was a word nobody used anymore, at least that's what Sami Rashwan told Shamika Johnson after she called him a dirty Moslem dicklick when he burped his way through *I Sing the Body Electric* in special chorus. My mother used other words that nobody said anymore, things like *coloreds* and *grody*. It was grody, for example, when her and Mac had sex on the waterbed in the room next to mine. I tuned the alarm-clock radio to AM static and held it against my ear while the mattress slapped against the bed frame with the patter of a wet fart. You had to sometimes burp a waterbed mattress to reduce air buildup and unnecessary noise. You had to sometimes condition it for I don't know what reason. This maintenance was easy to neglect and was why I was not allowed a waterbed, and why hers eventually sprung a leak that voided the lease and shorted out the downstairs lady's TVCR.

My mother said I was lucky because that last apartment was shit anyway, and our new one had central air and no bulldykes living downstairs. I was lucky to have a real home with a sliding-glass door that led to a backyard I never used because the neighbor's eighteen or so children infested it with their head lice and gummy Care Bear entrails. I was lucky to have a real home even if I had to wear fake Reeboks on my feet, and if I wanted to keep that roof over my head then I'd best not be asking for those authentic sixty-dollar Nikes Sue Applebaum was wearing.

I never found out what Slatora meant in Albanian, but in American it meant that by ninth grade it would become Slut-whora and that my shoes would always come from racks in Caldors instead of in boxes at Lady Foot Locker. I tried to make up a nickname, Tori, but my mother wouldn't let it stick and anyway, it wouldn't really mean anything different. Meanwhile Edward Donalds got to go by Mac, but that's just the kind of guy my mother would have as a boyfriend, someone who would give himself a name like that just so he could paint it on the cab of his truck. Sue Applebaum had to go by Sue Fattybum, and I was lucky, she said, because at least the name I was called implied people wanted to have sex with me.

No matter how many times I rode my bike the mile and a half to the Applebaums' house, I pulled up huffing to their street and had to rest a few minutes so I wouldn't seem out of shape when I got to their driveway. The Applebaums all called me skinny, but that was only because they were all as fat as their names made them sound: Sue and Stacey Fattybum and their parents, Dora and Samuel Fattybum. Samuel Applebaum was not fat in the same genetic way as his wife and daughters, just round in the belly from egg noodles and long bouts of unemployment. He was waxing his Dodge Daytona when I walked my bike into their driveway, wearing the fingerless driving gloves that served the same purpose as the bra on his car: none.

"Hey, Slatora," Mr. Applebaum said when I rolled my bike past him into the garage. "She's looking good, is she not?"

The Applebaums were people who said things like "Is she not?" instead of "Isn't she?" They got agita instead of stomachaches.

"Yeah, she's looking real good. Real shiny," I said.

"Well, don't just think you can walk by me without giving me a hug, pretty lady. We will be feeding you tonight, will we not?"

I leaned my bike against the cement wall and walked back to Mr. Applebaum. He pressed his chest against my face and planted his lips on the top of my head. He wore Avon cologne that came in bottles shaped like pistols and spark plugs, and he tucked his pastel polo shirt into his pastel slacks like an off-duty police officer. Mr. Applebaum was actually a former police officer, retired a few years before Sue was born. *Retired* was the word they used instead of *discharged under circumstances not discussed in the Applebaum house.* Mr. Applebaum was also a retired Radio Shack manager, ADT salesman, and part-time community college recruiter. He slid his hand to the small of my back, his pinky resting on the thick elastic waist of the peach Hanes Her Ways that crept up past my jeans.

"Man, I have to pee," I said and pulled away.

"Too much information," he said, although Mr. Applebaum often peed with the bathroom door opened a crack. Sometimes Pepe, their cocker spaniel, nosed his way through while Mr. Applebaum stood over the toilet, and Mr. Applebaum pretended not to hear the creak of the door on its hinges. Sometimes he whistled while he peed, sometimes he coughed. Sometimes he turned on the waterproof radio they kept in the shower, and that was something I envied the Applebaums for: that waterproof shower radio, the unexpected indulgences tucked into the musky corners of their house, the feeling that everyone everywhere was entitled to a little something special.

When I went inside, Sue was wearing Stacey's Ministry T-shirt. *The Land of Rape and Honey.*

"Stacey let you wear that?" I asked Sue.

"For three bucks and a back massage," she said. "And I have to do her dishes all week."

Sue didn't fill it out like Stacey. Sue was that rare kind of fat: fat and flat, no giant breasts to balance out the kangaroo-pooch of her stomach. Mrs. Applebaum told Sue her boobs would come and the weight would go. She'd bought Sue the Deal-a-Meal system from television, and Sue shuffled through the cards as if that was all there was to it. The Applebaums were people who bought things from television: Deal-a-Meal cards, Time-Life music compilations, juicers. I could die from want walking through that house.

"So what do you want to do tonight?" Sue asked.

I shrugged. "Go to the Athenian?" I asked. The Athenian IV was a Greek diner run by Albanians who winked their eyes at any girl over thirteen who entered. Sue's mother let us go there because she knew we knew better, while my mother would never let me near it since that was where she'd met my father.

"I'll see if my mom will drive us later," Sue said, although Mrs. Applebaum always drove us wherever we wanted to go, and later, of course, she did.

"I'll come back around ten thirty to pick you up," Mrs. Applebaum said when we pulled up to the neon sign that lit the way to the entrance.

"Eleven," Sue said.

"Ten thirty," Mrs. Applebaum said. "I can't stay up all night waiting for you. Besides, what are you going to do in a diner for two and a half hours? Now give me a kiss."

Sue rolled her eyes about the ten-thirty pick-up time but not about the kiss. That she planted on her mother's cheek with a loud *mwah*, the sound the Applebaums would have you think every kiss naturally made. The Applebaums hugged in big round-the-waist squeezes that kept your lungs from taking in new air until they finally released you with a groan that sounded like their kisses: mwah. I thought mwah could've been a word I didn't know, a Hebrew one like the others they'd taught me. Shalom. L'chaim. To life, the last one meant. Shalom meant hello, goodbye, and peace. I used to wonder how people knew which meaning someone actually intended when they said it, but Sue rolled her eyes when I asked her.

"Context clues," she said, which made it sound like we were playing school instead of whatever it was we were actually playing.

Inside, the host asked us if we wanted smoking or non.

"Smoking," Sue said, even though we didn't have anything to smoke. The old ladies who smoked Misti 100s by the inch stubbed their butts into hard elbows when they saw girls like us, as if the very idea of us could steal the joy from cigarettes. We flipped through the menus the host placed down on the table, but we would just order coffee and gravy fries like usual. We only looked through the menu so we could wonder aloud who ate the stuff.

"Salisbury steak?" Sue said. "I bet it's Stouffer's."

"Lookit, chicken cacciatore. It's like, a fried chicken wing with some American cheese on it."

"Chicken cacciatore? Is that what you want?" a waitress asked over our shoulders.

"No, just coffee. Do you want some fries?" Sue asked me.

"Um, I don't know. If you do I'll eat some."

"I'm only going to eat a few," Sue said.

"Me too."

"And some gravy fries," Sue told the waitress. The waitress came back a minute later with cups half-full of coffee. She left space for plenty of creamer, like we always drank it. Light and sweet, like us, Mr. Applebaum said. He called his girls *sweetie* unless he was mad. When he was mad he shouted and called everyone by their proper names, everyone except me.

"I'm sorry about this, sweetie," he'd say to me. "All this yelling around you."

The Applebaums were people who yelled hard and apologized later. They weren't people who shut themselves away for days at a time, pot smoke crawling out from beneath hollow doorframes like silverfish.

"Could you get the waitress to bring some more cream? We're going to run out in like, four seconds," I said. "Man, I have to pee."

"Too much information," Sue said.

I got up from the table and wound my way around the loose chairs strewn about like roadblocks in the smoking section. Smokers didn't get booths with mini jukeboxes mounted into the walls. They didn't get to play Genesis or Joe Walsh. Life hadn't been good to them so far, which was why they were smokers. Still, they weren't as bad off as the men who sat alone in the swivel chairs at the counter. Those men ate pies from the glass dessert case and leered at girls passing by on their way to the bathroom. I walked the furthest path around them that I could but eventually had to swing close to them to get to the ladies room, which was planted so near the counter that every girl who had to pee could smell the Copenhagen on their breath as they let out grunts that approved of the best asses passing by.

"Slatora," somebody called when I reached the door. I turned my head toward my name believing that no one at that counter should have known it, but I saw then that I was wrong: I had earned a place among them. Mac Donalds grinned at me from four feet away, his pink tongue an earthworm crawling through the space where his right canine should have been.

"Hi," I said. The oval patch on the chest of his coveralls spelled his name in a cursive close to calligraphy, like an invitation to a wedding nobody wanted to go to. He held a Pall Mall between his lips as he spoke.

"Your mother know you're here?" he asked.

I shrugged. "I guess. It's not like it's a bar."

"It's worse. These are the guys got kicked out of the bar."

At home, Mac slept till noon on the weekends but was out the door before sunrise on weekdays. We rarely spoke. I just heard the grunts and creaks of the new box spring on the other side of the wall and kept my door closed until I left for the Applebaums'. I know he watched our television while we were gone because he spotted the sofa with change and sunflower seeds that had fallen out of his pocket, as if he had to leave a trail to find again the place that he'd left. My mother collected the change and dropped it into a bowl that she turned in for paper bills once a month. *I sure as hell earned this*, she'd say.

"Where's my mother?" I asked him. I just wanted to make sure she wasn't there.

"Kicked my ass out of there tonight," he said. "You hear about what happened?"

I shook my head.

"Big news, kid. I found a dead body on my truck route this afternoon. It's gonna be all over the news tonight. Don't you watch the news? You should be watching the news instead of all them soap opera pieces of trash."

I'd never watched a soap in my life. "You found a body?" I said. Instantly she flashed in front of me: a swollen woman shawled in gauzy white, as if the she'd planned ahead what to wear for the best effect. Or maybe she was naked. Maybe Mac stared at her nipples the way he stared at my mother's when she wore his curdled tank tops without a bra.

Mac choked out something that was supposed to be a laugh, but from the way his eyes jumped from mine to the ashtray to the exit sign humming red over the door I knew he didn't mean anything funny. He changed his mind because he knew it wasn't working and coughed instead, and a tiny black cinder floated down from his cigarette like a mosquito slapped dead on a forearm and flicked aside. "Well, parts of it anyway. Bunch of *parts* of a dead body."

"Oh my god," I said. I didn't want to talk to Mac, not then or ever, but dead bodies have a way of making you want to know about them, these people you never gave a shit about in actual life. "Where? How?"

"Out on 73, you know that real freaky road kind of near the old Watertown drive-in? Over that area," he said. The Watertown drive-in had shut down before I could ever watch a movie there, the broad white screens still propped up on poles like sails on a boat that had run a hundred miles ashore. Only people that went down that way were drunk teenagers on ATVs and the men who met at Maxie's Café, the gay bar someone stashed away in a place where wives would never think to look for their husbands' pickups. "Yeah, I mean, all hacked up. I literally fucking tripped over an arm sticking out of a cereal box. Fruity Pebbles. Fucking funny, right? Fruity Pebbles, yabba fucking dabba do. Excuse my French, Slatora. Kind of shaken up still."

I still saw the woman in white, tucked bit by bit into boxes. "I don't understand," I said, "you tripped over them how? Were they just in the middle of the road or something?"

He exhaled so much smoke through his nose that I wondered how his nose hair didn't catch fire. "Christ, you sound like your mother. No, they were in the woods. I had to take a piss, if you need to know that much."

I shook my head. I didn't. At least at home Mac peed with the door closed, although his stream was so loud that it carried through the two rooms between the bathroom and my bedroom. "But who was it? I mean, what . . ."

"Slatora, I don't know anything more than you do. I'll be watching the news myself to find out what the hell's going on." He shook his head. "Great start to the weekend, I'll tell you that much."

There were more questions I wanted to ask him, the last of which would have been, Why did my mother kick you out for finding a dead body? But Mac had turned his attention to the waitress refilling his coffee, and I knew that to mean conversation over. I started to walk away, and then Mac cocked his head back in my direction. "Don't worry, I won't tell your mother you were here," he said.

It was supposed to make us friends, I think, but it only made me forget that I'd gone over there in the first place to pee. I pivoted on my heel instead and rushed back to the table, where Sue sat twirling a thin piece of hair that'd fallen out of her ponytail. She barely looked up when I sat back down, but I knew she was glad that I was there. Sitting together in the smoking section felt powerful, but alone it was a reminder of why we should never let ourselves grow up to drink coffee by ourselves in a room lit entirely with neon.

"Holy crap, guess what?" I said as I dropped back into my seat. "I just saw my mom's boyfriend Mac over there by the counter. He found a dead body this afternoon. All hacked up into little pieces and stuffed in cereal boxes."

"What?" Sue said. She was envious of what I'd just said, I knew, the same way I envied that Ministry T-shirt. "What are you talking about?"

"Yeah, he found a murdered person. He says it's going to be on the news tonight."

"Oh my God," Sue said. "That's *crazy*. Who was it? Where did he find it?"

"I don't know," I said to both questions, which meant I was only lying about one. "He didn't want to talk about it. He said just to watch the news."

"What time is it?" Sue checked her watch. "Well, I want to catch the ten o'clock, then. I'll call my mom to tell her to pick us up early." She got up from the table and slipped out to the use the lobby payphone. While I sat alone, I sipped my coffee and the waitress brought out the plate of fries we'd ordered. I pulled one from the bottom of the pile and slipped it into my mouth, swallowing the last of it before Sue came back to the table.

"She's going to come in a half an hour," she said. "Why aren't you eating yet?"

"I'm just not that hungry," I said. The salt of the gravy still coated the roof of my mouth, and I ran my tongue along it to collect the residual stew collected in the ridges.

"I hate you. You're so skinny," she said.

I rolled my eyes, but inside I felt the blood pumping fast through my veins, egged on by caffeine and joy.

I was wrong about the body. There was no white dress. There was no lady at all. The newswoman said the parts had not yet been identified but that they likely belonged to a city contractor who'd been missing for weeks. Police were investigating the possibility that the murder was mafia-related.

"Damn guineas," Mr. Applebaum said. He stood over the couch through the entire story, poised to act should the phone ring and he be called out of police retirement.

"Now that's not necessary," Mrs. Applebaum said. "We've got all different types in this room and we're not going to encourage hate speech. Slatora is a Muslim, don't forget."

"My mother says Moslem," I said.

"It's basically the same thing," Mrs. Applebaum said. "You say tomato, I say tomahto."

"No you don't," Sue said. "I never heard you say tomahto."

"I'm just trying to make a point. There are a lot of different ways to say the same thing," Mrs. Applebaum said.

"Edward Donalds is your mother's boyfriend? What was he doing out on Route 73?" Mr. Applebaum asked.

"He drives a linen truck. I guess he was out delivering linens," I said.

"Delivering them in the woods behind Maxie's? There's only one thing that place uses linens for, and it's not for cleaning up coffee spills, if you catch my drift."

"Samuel, stop talking like that! Slatora is not her mother's boy-friend's keeper."

"He said he was in the woods to pee," I said. "And he tripped over an arm."

"Was there anybody with him?" Mr. Applebaum asked.

"I don't think so," I said. "He didn't say anything about it."

Mr. Applebaum laughed a laugh that was supposed to be quiet, like he wanted to keep it to himself, but of course we all heard it. "Stop it, Sam," Mrs. Applebaum said. "There are kids here."

"We're not kids," Sue said.

"You're *our* kids," Mrs. Applebaum said. She sat between me and Sue on the couch and squeezed both of our thighs. "Always."

The Applebaums were always hugging and kissing and squeezing thighs. They'd taken the *honorary* out of my title and made me into one of their kids, Sue and Stacey and now Slatora. I even kept the alliteration going, an effect of a poet. The Applebaums were people who might even know what alliteration meant, unlike my mother, who laughed at the word *assonance* written on one of my English papers.

"Assonance," she'd said. "I'll kick your assonance good."

My mother sounded like she wanted to kick my assonance good when she called the Applebaums a half hour later.

"Where the hell are you? Did I give you permission to spend the night there?" she said.

I brought the cordless phone down the half-flight of steps into the basement of their split-level so the Applebaums wouldn't hear me. "I don't know. I don't usually need permission to spend the night here. I do it all the time."

"Well it's about time you get some rules. You need to starting asking me before you leave this house."

"It's not a house," I said. "It's an apartment."

"Don't get smart with me. A house is just wherever you live."

I wanted to argue but there'd be no point.

"And I want you back here now," she said.

My heart dropped down to my generic Reeboks. "But why? I'm just at Sue's. Why are you making such a big deal suddenly?"

"Because I'm sick of you people treating me like an idiot is why," she said. "You and Mac both think I'm stupid."

"I don't have anything to do with Mac," I said. "He's your boyfriend, not mine. I barely even know him." I didn't mention the conversation at the Athenian. I didn't mention the ten o'clock news.

"Yeah, well that makes two of us then. I didn't know I was dating a cocksucker either."

I kept quiet.

"Never told me he was a fag," she said.

I kept quiet.

"What are you, a mute?" she said. "Say something."

"How do you know he's a fag?" I asked.

She snorted. "Watch the news, then tell me what he's doing out in the woods behind Maxie's. You know what the pile of mattresses behind that place is used for, right? Or do you? God, you're so naïve, Slatora. It's about time you grew up."

"I know what the mattresses are for," I said, even though I'd just then figured it out. They were used for the same thing hers was. I could see my mother there, through the phone: her limbs splayed over the bed like unwanted things, things she constantly shooed away. She wanted other people to take them in, like foster children.

"Well aren't you a baby Einstein," she said. "Now get your ass home." The phone clicked back into a dial tone, but I held onto it for another minute while I blinked back tears. Finally I headed back upstairs.

"What's going on?" Mr. Applebaum said. "Why are your eyes all glassy? Everything alright?"

"Yeah," I said. "My throat's just dry or something."

Sue's room held two identical canopy beds that she'd outgrown, but the Applebaums kept them so I'd have my own bed to sleep in. Me and Sue draped ourselves over the mattresses with *Seventeen* magazines spread out in front of us, her with the newest November and me with October, which I'd already read three times over the month. We both flipped through the pages too quickly to even pretend that we were reading them, until finally Sue looked up.

"I can't believe Mac found some guy all hacked up like that," she said.

"I know," I said. "For some reason, when he first told me about it I thought it was a woman. I always picture dead bodies being women."

"You're weird," Sue said. "Of course guys get killed. Probably more than women."

"I know. It's just how I picture them," I said.

I imagined my mother at home, lying among bedsheets that hadn't been washed or made in months, her nipples poking out from Mac's tank top like tiny pebbles under a blanket. You could trace a chalk line around her sometimes, the way she lay on her back for hours. Then it would all go to hell when she got up and slammed a coffee mug so hard into the sink that ceramic pieces splintered off like sharp teeth and fell into the drain. Then she'd curse and break another one when the teeth bit into her skin when she tried to clear the clog. She might show up at the Applebaums soon, if she was mad enough. But probably not. Probably it'd be best to wait it out until the morning, when she'd pull her legs around as if they'd been cast in cement.

"Your mom sounded pissed when she called," Sue said. "Is she upset about it or something?"

"I don't know," I said. "I don't ever know what she's upset about," I lied. I always had some idea, or many ideas that were all, I think, a little bit right.

"Your mom's even weirder than you are. No offense," Sue said. "You know I love you because you're weird."

"You're weird too," I said. "You have two canopy beds in your room. You gave your sister a back massage to wear her Ministry T-shirt."

"And three dollars," she reminded me.

"And you're Jewish," I said.

"You're Moslem," she said.

"Your mom says tomahto," I said.

"Your mom named you Slut-whora."

"She wants me to take after her," I said.

"I wish my mom had named me something slutty instead of something fatty. Now I'm stuck with this big gut."

"I've never even kissed anybody," I said. "So obviously the name doesn't have anything to do with it," I said.

"I'll trade you anyway," she said.

"Gladly," I said, only I wonder if Sue knew I wasn't after her name.

The Applebaums were all blessed with insomnia. Stacey got to stay out until dawn at the Tune Inn in New Haven, spilling out of her room the next afternoon reeking of cigarettes and other people's sweat and the Sharpie marker that blacked in her fingernails, a perfume that Sue and I could only dream of wearing. The rest of the Applebaums stayed up for Arsenio and infomercials. I took my place on the loveseat between Mrs. Applebaum and Sue, eating Moon Pies and drinking pink lemonade to stay awake.

"That Bronson Pinchot is so talented," Mrs. Applebaum said after we watched him on Arsenio. Or "Wow, that stuff really works," after DD7 dissolved a pool of red wine from a white carpet. It worked also on rust. Grape juice. Pet stains. Blood.

"Wonder if that guinea used DD7 to clean up after he sawed apart that city contractor," Mr. Applebaum said.

"Sam, I'm not going to say it again. This is probably very upsetting to Slatora. How do you think Sue would feel if one of us had found a dead body?"

"He's just my mom's boyfriend," I said. "I don't really care that much."

"Even so. It's a human being we're talking about. He deserves a little respect."

"Actually, he's kind of gross. I think my Mom broke up with him tonight."

"I was talking about the dead person," Mrs. Applebaum said.

"Oh," I said.

Mr. Applebaum laughed. "No offense to your mother, sweetie, but it doesn't sound like Mac is the kind of guy you'd want around, anyway. Just from my time on the force, I knew about the guys that hung out around Route 73. Not the cream of the crop."

"I know," I said. "I don't get to choose my mother's boyfriends, though."

"Exactly. Leave her alone, Sam. She doesn't have anything to do with Edward Donalds, and neither does her mother anymore, so let' s just leave it at that."

Mr. Applebaum ignored Mrs. Applebaum. "You know, Slatora, you're welcome to stay here if you'd like. On a more permanent basis, I mean, if things aren't, you know, that *great* at home," Mr. Applebaum said.

I nodded my head but didn't say anything. It seemed speaking would make me seem desperate, for me to say that things were not that *great* at home, although I appreciated how Mr. Applebaum put things, in terms of what things weren't instead of what they were. Mrs. Applebaum and Sue didn't say anything at all, but I could tell from the way they stared at the screen with expressionless faces that this was something they'd talked about before. My eyes watered over again.

"The heat in here is so dry," I said. "God, my throat. I'm going to go put on my pajamas."

I walked quickly down the hallway to Sue's room. She kept a T-shirt and a pair of boxers she'd outgrown two years ago in the top drawer of her white bureau for me to wear whenever I slept over. I pulled them out but just hugged them to my chest because really I'd just gone in there to cry where no one could see me. I would come back in ten minutes saying that I'd gotten caught up reading *Seventeen*. I'd have brushed my teeth and washed my face and said that I'd gotten soap in my eyes. Red eyes, all that dry heat. But as I sat down on the canopy bed, Mr. Applebaum pushed open the door to Sue's bedroom and then closed it shut behind him again. I let the tear that slid down my cheek just drop from my chin onto the nightshirt, because by then I'd run out of other things to do.

Mr. Applebaum sat next to me. "Do you want to talk about anything?" he asked.

I shook my head.

"Do you want to stay here with us?" he asked.

I shrugged.

"I know things are tough for you," he said. "But you're lucky that you have a friend like Sue. You're lucky that we all love you. Some people don't have anything."

"I know," I said. "I know I'm lucky." My mother said it—lucky. Sue said it—lucky. I was a high roller, making all these somethings out of nothing.

"We'll make a place for you. You're a very beautiful young woman," he said.

I didn't say anything because I thought that would be conceited.

"Very beautiful," he said again. "Can I have a hug?"

I pulled in close to his chest. I think the cologne had gone bad. Those bottles had all sat on his dresser for years, and the musk and wood had long been swallowed by alcohol.

"You need any help changing into your nightclothes?" he asked.

I shook my head.

"I'm kidding, Slatora. You know I'm kidding." He smiled, and the tongue that crawled out from his lips looked soft and cold as an earthworm, like the one that'd been crawling out of Mac's lips a few hours before at the Athenian, as if Mac had bit down on it and it had regenerated, and then I'd carried the new part from one place to the next. Those were the things you could pick up on damp mattresses in woods: earthworms, things that crawled inside of bodies and churned them into dirt. They regenerated when you tried to cut them into pieces, and suddenly they were everywhere. They didn't even need each other to live. They didn't need anything, only really they did.

"I have to use the bathroom," I said.

"I'm glad you didn't say you have to pee," Mr. Applebaum said. "It's not becoming."

I brought the nightshirt and boxers into the bathroom with me and changed into them in there. I washed my face and gargled with Listerine and sat on the toilet for a few minutes, the radio in the shower on but soft, so only I could hear it.

By the time I went back to the living room, Mr. Applebaum had taken his place on the La-Z-Boy. Mrs. Applebaum and Sue moved their feet off the cushion where I'd been sitting before I got up to change.

"We were keeping it warm for you," Sue said, and I sat down without saying anything.

What I wanted to do was say many things, tell a story laid out in pieces like a corpse tucked in cereal boxes, if only I could get the different parts to imply one whole thing. I wanted to tell Sue that in two days Mac would again be in bed with my mother, the static on my alarm-clock radio turned so loud they will bang on the wall to get me to turn it down until my mother storms in, swearing, and rips it from my hands. I wanted to warn her away from a life that in four years would uproot her to New Haven with Stacey, working as a telephone operator by day, passing Sharpie markers and ashtrays to each other in a condo financed by the double indemnity paid out after the Metro-North commuter train kissed hard the Daytona that had somehow stalled on the tracks, Mr. Applebaum found inside still gripping the wheel. I wanted to tell her that in fifteen years Mrs. Applebaum will run into people at the IGA and always, without being asked, tell them all about her girls. I wanted to tell her thank you for keeping the seat warm for me.

All of the ways to say the same thing, and dear God, I could never even come up with one.

The Kill Jar

Mom thinks I'm going to be a poet. She says, "Oh, that's Kevin Jr. He's going to be a *poet*," and she smiles like she does at the retarded people she drives around in the white van, and then she pats me on the head. But I don't even like poetry. It's only because in third grade I wrote a poem that went like this—

Puppy black and white
You bring so much joy to me
You are my puppy

—when we were learning about haikus, and some kids in my class were so stupid they didn't understand syllables so they couldn't write them. They couldn't get it even when Miss Hitt broke it down to Sy-La-Bull with hand claps in between, which is why I hate being in the dumb class because I'm not dumb like those kids. I mean, Dr. Imperioli says I'm bright and just have trouble with *focus* and *attention*, and that's not dumb, that's just lazy Mom says. Anyway, I don't even have a dog because Mom says I'm not responsible enough, but when Miss Hitt read the poem she wrote a note to Miss Herr, my second grade teacher, and she had me walk it down the hall to Miss Herr and I read it along the way. The note said, "Kevin has outdone himself!!!" and there was a gold star next to it. And then Miss Herr wrote a note to my mom and now Mom always says,

"Oh, that's Kevin Jr. He's going to be a *poet*," except when Old Dad is around he says, "You mean he's going to be a homo?" and Mom laughs and pats me on the head again.

But what I'm really going to be is an entomologist, which is a scientist who studies insects. I just figured that out this summer because I've been studying insects, which at first was because I had to for school, because in fifth grade the science teacher Mr. Baronowski makes everybody hand in a bug collection with thirty bugs pinned to a Styrofoam sheet and labeled in typing if possible or very neat handwriting if not. So in the summer before fifth grade everybody starts capturing bugs on their own because there's more bugs in summer to capture, and the rich kids with pools just scoop them out of the pools already dead, which is cheating I think.

But I don't even need a pool. Actual Dad helped me cheat a little bit though, but just that once. He came to pick me up at the Y and he said, "Hey Kevin Jr., I got something for you," and he pulled out a plastic baggie from his work cooler. Inside the baggie was a butterfly that turned out to be a Mourning Cloak Butterfly I found out later. It still moved a little bit in the bag, just kind of a little in its wings, real slow, like maybe the wind could have been doing it, but since there was no wind in the plastic baggie I guess it had to be the butterfly itself. It was mostly maroon except for a yellow outline and tiny white dots around the outline, and there was a little tear in its right wing. The Mourning Cloak Butterfly probably didn't feel it tear but it probably flapped and flapped its wings wondering why doing that didn't make it fly anymore, except butterflies probably don't even think, but I feel like everything must a little or else how is it even alive?

"It was hanging outside the shop," Actual Dad said, "on the ground outside the door. Figured you could use it since the work's pretty much done on it already."

"Thanks," I said, even though I like doing the work on my own, because I know he was just trying to help. I figured I could probably find one without a tear in its wing later but I didn't tell him that.

"Guess Your Mother's not going to help too much on this. Such a woman when it comes to bugs," he said. Actual Dad calls her Your Mother now. It's hard for me to keep up with all these names for everybody, so I just stopped calling most of them by name at all except for in my head. Like Mom is still Mom to me but not to Actual Dad, and Dad isn't Dad to me anymore but Actual Dad, but to Mom he's Your Other Dad and to Old Dad he's Kevin Sr., and Grandpa isn't Grandpa to me anymore but Old Dad since Mom married him, but Mom calls him Your New Dad and Actual Dad doesn't call him anything at all. Usually I just say "Hey" when I want somebody's attention.

"I have to keep them under my bed in case she comes in for something," I told him. "One time I showed her a dead yellow jacket and she started crying."

"Yup," Actual Dad said, but I don't think he even heard me because he was looking real hard out the window like he was reading something even though the only thing out there was a billboard of a lady in a glittery dress smoking a cigarette as skinny as she was. Then he pulled out a Coors Light from the cooler where the butterfly was and took a swig and then he wasn't staring anymore. "Well, fuck her, then," and he gave me the beer to hold onto like he showed me, underneath the window so people outside the truck can't see it. "You should stick a whole nest in that bitch's bed."

He'd say stuff like that and I'd laugh because I figured he was just joking.

I did something I wasn't supposed to do. It's because we live in Connecticut or otherwise it would be okay. But Mr. Baronowski said we weren't supposed to capture Praying Mantises because it's the official state insect of Connecticut. But where I usually captured bugs, which was at the Mad River across the street from our apartment, I didn't see any I didn't already have. I have twenty-two bumblebees in case they crumble because sometimes they get crispy when they're dead and fall apart when you're trying to

The Kill Jar / 21

pin them through their thorax. I have so many beetles I can't even count them. I have a dozen ladybugs and I could have more, but my mother says it's bad luck to kill them. So I was down at the riverbank and all I saw were those things and some centipedes and stuff under rocks but they're not really insects, they're anthropods. And then I looked up at a leaf and it wasn't a leaf at all. It was green like a leaf and was kind of tear-drop shaped like a leaf, but I knew it was a praying mantis right away because I've gotten so good at spotting bugs, which is why I think I should be an entomologist.

And then it looked right at me. It turned its head like a hundred degrees, which I've never seen an insect do before, and it looked right at me like I called out its name or something. So I did. I said, "Hey praying manty wanty," and it didn't do anything except keep staring at me like maybe it had never seen a human person before. I kept whispering to it and stepping closer a little bit at a time, and I was about to close it in between the kill jar and the lid, but I didn't want to kill it, just capture it, so I dumped out the cotton balls and then, real real slow, surrounded the praying mantis and got it.

Old Dad was lying in the living room when I ran in through the door because he blew his knee out and can't work for a while, and usually he's sleeping because the medication makes him sleepy, especially if he drinks beer with it, but he was awake then and he said, "Whoa buddy, this ain't a race track." I slowed down so he wouldn't have any more reason to talk to me.

"Hold on, buddy," he said anyway. "What you got there?"

I didn't know if he knew I wasn't supposed to capture praying mantises so at first I didn't want to show him, but then I didn't think he would care because I've seen him do stuff he's not supposed to do like pee with the door open and I never told on him. So I handed him the jar and the praying mantis looked right at him too.

"He's a big fucker," Old Dad said, and then he flicked the glass, which I wished he wouldn't do.

"She," I said. I knew it was a she because they're bigger than the men and this one was about four inches long.

"She's a big ol' bitch, then," he said. "Better kill her quick before your mom gets home."

"Uh-huh," I said, and then I walked into my room. But I didn't want to kill her because she didn't even seem like a bug to me since she was so big and could look around and everything. Plus, he can't really tell me what to do and his breath smells so bad my brain goes dizzy when he talks to me, plus Mom told me to ignore him when he uses bad words. So I went into the hall closet and took out the little fishbowl that Mom used to try to keep fish in except they always died so she gave up, and I turned the jar upside down into the fishbowl and dropped the praying mantis in. I covered the top with the knee-high pantyhose I had in my room from when I put it over my head and made Mom laugh so hard she blew beer out of her nose and then cried 'cause it burned so bad, which made me laugh harder when she did that until Old Dad smacked me for laughing at Mom while she cried. And then I just studied the praying mantis for a while. I watched her move her head around and rub her hands together like she was a villain with an evil plan to take over the universe. I decided to name her Melissa. Melissa didn't seem to mind the bowl or even care because she wasn't fighting back or anything, and I figured as long as I put some leaves and twigs in there she might not even realize she was somewhere she wasn't supposed to be.

I don't like it when Mom brings the retards home. Like Jimmy that day, he's a big black retard who kept trying to hug me but he smelled like scalloped potatoes and I hate scalloped potatoes. So I tried to get away but he was giant and weighed like three hundred pounds.

"He's just trying to be nice," Mom said, but I think she just wanted him to hug me so he wouldn't hug her because I saw her elbow him in the chest last time he tried to touch her.

"He smells," I said.

"Jimmy, you getting ripe?" she said.

"I don't want anybody crapping themselves in my kitchen," Old Dad yelled out from the living room.

"He didn't crap himself, he just can't clean himself real good," Mom yelled back. "I do recall wiping your ass a few times myself, gimpy."

"Dammit, I'd shove my foot upside your ass if I wasn't already down to one good leg," Old Dad said.

They were just playing because they both laughed, but Jimmy I guess didn't know that and let go of me and started this orangutan moan and slapped himself on the face real hard over and over again. I mean *hard*. I can't believe some human beings are so stupid that they hurt themselves on purpose and then cry because they're hurt, but that stuff happens all the time when they're around.

"Why don't you bring them somewhere else?" I said.

"You want to pay for me to eat lunch somewhere *else* every day? You want to start doing your own laundry because I'm somewhere *else* every day?"

"I don't care," I said because those were stupid questions anyway.

"Then why don't *you* go somewhere else?" she said.

"Fine," I said, and I went to my room because it was the only somewhere else I could go. She was about to smoke a marijuana cigarette anyway, and I know she's not supposed to do that even if she says doctors give it out to sick people so how can it be that bad?

When I walked in, Melissa was sitting on a twig I'd stuffed in her bowl. The bug book said that praying mantises are named that because it looks like they're praying, but I think it looks more like a dog sitting up to beg for food. So then I realized she must be hungry. I can be so stupid sometimes, like of course she's hungry, wouldn't I be hungry if I didn't eat all day? The book said she was a carnivore, which means she eats bugs and other alive things, but I forgot to get any alive bugs for her. Stupid stupid stupid. Except then I remembered the butterfly Actual Dad gave me and I went to check if it was still alive in the baggie. It still kind of was, like it still pulsed its wings a little bit when I flicked the baggie, and its wings were pretty so I felt bad for a second that I was going to feed it to the praying mantis for dinner. But it was probably going to die anyway, and even if it did live it wouldn't be able to fly and what was the point of a walking butterfly?

Melissa didn't move or anything, didn't even turn her head, so I thought maybe butterflies were gross to her like scalloped potatoes are gross to me. But then ZAP! so fast, she grabbed onto the butterfly and pulled it tight and just munched right through its neck, and the butterfly's wings pulsed faster for a few seconds and then stopped altogether.

"There," I told the butterfly. It's a trick they have, that butterflies try to look like flowers so that enemies won't eat them. Obviously it doesn't work.

"You're going to come live with me, Kevin Jr."

That's what Actual Dad said the next day when he picked me up at the Y.

"Okay," I said, but I didn't really believe him because he's been saying that since him and Mom got divorced. At least Actual Dad wouldn't sleep on the couch all the time and fart so loud it wakes him up.

"You can't be living like that," he said. "It's not natural."

"Yeah," I said, but I got kind of mad because maybe he was making fun of me or something. I don't like that Mom married Grandpa, but it's not what they say it is. Like the kids at school call me Incest is Best. They say incest is when people in the same family hump each other, but Mom and Old Dad aren't really related, Actual Dad and Old Dad are. The kids at school are too stupid to even know that since they couldn't even count syllables in third grade, but I thought Actual Dad would at least understand it.

"That man . . . nope. Not with my kid, he's not."

I didn't say anything this time because I don't think he was talking to me even though I was the only other person in the truck. He was looking sideways and talking so quiet I could barely hear him.

"And her. And her," I think he said.

I noticed a tiny grasshopper on the windshield of the truck. It crawled from the top all the way to the windshield wipers at the bottom of the window, which must have been hard with all that wind blowing on it. It was so small I didn't think it would be a good dinner for Melissa, but maybe it could be a snack.

"Hey, Kevin," he said, way louder so I knew he actually was talking to me. "You been taking your medication?"

"Mom says I don't need it anymore."

"That's not what Dr. Imperioli thinks," he said. "Or your teachers."

I didn't answer because I don't care what the teachers think.

"So you don't need it, then who's taking it? Because someone's taking it. Because I'm still paying for it."

I shrugged. The grasshopper looked right at me like it knew what was up.

"You know what that stuff is, right? Ritalin? You know what it does?"

"Nope," I said. *We're going to get you, grasshopper*, I thought.

"It's your mother taking it," he said.

"So," I said.

"So what does she act like?" he said. "At home. What does Your Mother and everybody do?"

"Um, she comes home and makes food. She always brings retards with her. I hate them," I said. *And I hate you*, I thought to the grass-hopper, even though I didn't really. I was just trying to hunt it.

"She still smoke pot?" he asked.

"Guess so," I said.

"You hang around at all?"

"Not really. I don't like the retards." *You will be our captive.*

"The retards stay, though?"

"I guess so," I said. "Till they have to go home."

He got real soft and turned sideways again. "Fucker," he said, and then he mumbled too bad for me to even hear him, so I just stopped listening and stared at the grasshopper. Its antennae were waving all over the place from the wind but its legs were stuck on the glass like cement. I bet it'd be cool to be able to stick to things like that, walk up walls and everything.

Actual Dad pulled into my parking lot but he didn't hit the brakes hard to skid out on the sand like he usually does. "I'll see you tomorrow, Kevin," he said.

"It's not your day tomorrow," I told him.

"Nope," he said. "Not gonna be her day, either." Then he closed my door and took off so fast I couldn't even say good-bye. I didn't have time to grab Melissa's snack either.

Melissa is related to cockroaches. Like, cousins or something. That's what the book said anyway, but I don't really see how. We used to have cockroaches in our last apartment, but they were little and red and ugly and made Mom scream so loud that once the neighbors knocked on the door because they thought she was being stabbed. Then another time I found her on the floor curled up like the grubs me and Actual Dad go fishing with, and there was a bowl broken all over the floor and cereal everywhere and she was crying so hard she couldn't even make a sound until I asked her what was wrong and she screamed, "Fuck this place! Fuck it!" Finally when she calmed down she told me there was a roach in her cereal and that we shouldn't have to live like this if Your Father would just start paying some decent child support then we wouldn't have to live like this and fuck that man, fuck him fuck him fuck him. Then we moved in with Old Dad a little bit after that. His apartment was nicer and didn't have roaches so she didn't cry as much anymore.

So I feel bad I made her cry. It wasn't my fault, though, not really. Well maybe a little because I know she hates bugs and I wasn't supposed to keep any alive bugs in the house, but I didn't know she was going to come into my room like that. Melissa was lying on her twig on top of my desk, just waiting for me to feed her. I think I trained her 'cause she never tried to run or anything when I brought her out of the fishbowl, just sat there and rubbed her hands together and waited for the moth or beetle or whatever I got for her that day. And that day it was a cricket, a big, black, shiny one that I bet would've been delicious. I pulled the cricket out of the jar and dangled it in front of Melissa, and then I dropped it and shielded them both with my hands so that the cricket wouldn't hop away.

"Kevin, you got my nail-polish remover again?"

I didn't even hear Mom open the door, but then I turned around and she was standing there drumming the doorframe with her fingers.

"Uh, uh, no. Yeah," I said. I couldn't shield the cricket anymore or else she'd wonder what I was doing. I felt it jump up against my arm, then drop back down to who knows where.

"Yeah or no?" she asked, and then she came over to the desk to look for it herself. "Didn't I tell you I needed it back?"

"No, it's over here," I said, and I walked over to the closet even though it wasn't there but I wanted her to look away from the desk, except it was too late because then I heard it.

"Kk . . . Kyuh . . ." she said, like she was trying to say either "Kevin" or "Kill It" but that's all that would come out. "Ahhhh," she said, and it kept getting louder and louder until she was screaming her whole head off, and I know if I ever screamed that loud in the house I'd get in so much trouble and smacked in the mouth. She screamed so loud that Jimmy came running up behind her and nailed himself against the wall and made his orangutan noises until Old Dad finally hobbled in there and said, "What the Christ is going on here?"

Mom finally unfroze herself and ran over to the door where everybody was standing and fell down on her knees. "Bbb . . . Bug!" she said.

"Where at? Kevin, what I tell you about bringing bugs in here?" Old Dad said, and I tried to tell him I didn't but then he told me to shut my mouth like I was the one screaming. So I sat down on the floor behind Mom because I figured it was a better place to be, farther away from him.

"Go kill that thing," he said. I hated him so much right then I wanted to stuff him into a giant kill jar and choke him with nail polish remover and stick a giant pin through his gut. I would've stuck him to the wall and made a label that said "Old Butthead" and poked him with a needle until he crumbled and couldn't even be used for a collection anymore 'cause he'd be in too many pieces to be good for anything.

"Now," he said, and then picked me up, I guess because he knew I wouldn't move on my own, and pushed me over to the desk. I didn't see Melissa though. I guess she got scared and jumped off somewhere, which was what I wanted to do too, but she was so small there were just a lot more places for her to hide than for me to.

"She's not up here," I said.

"What's that, smartass?" he said, and he pointed down at the floor to the cricket.

"Oh," I said, and I crunched it with my shoe without thinking twice. It was just the cricket. I figured as long as Old Dad told her something was dead, Mom would be happy. And I was happy too, even though Melissa's dinner was gone because I knew I could find something else for her eventually.

"Dead," I said, and I picked up the cricket to show him.

"Good," he said. "It's dead, Irene," he said to Mom, and she nodded. Then after a minute Mom said to Jimmy, "It's fine now, Jimmy, stop hitting yourself like that," and she pulled down hard on his arms until he stopped hitting himself. Then everything was quiet again and I wished they'd all go.

"From now on that bug collection stays at Kevin Sr.'s house," Old Dad said, and then they all walked out just like I wished for. I also wish Mom had told me it was fine now like she told Jimmy, but whatever. I'm not a retard like he is.

Actual Dad was there to pick me up again at the Y, even though I told him the day before it wasn't his turn, it was Mom's turn.

"She's busy," he said when I asked him what he was doing there.

"Busy doing what?" I asked.

"Busy," he said, and I don't know what that meant but he said it in that voice he uses when I'm not supposed to talk back. I figured Mom was stuck working late with the retards, because sometimes they make her stay after she drops them off at the home and do some work there too, and she doesn't like it because she's got her own cooking and laundry to do, what do they think she just goes home and gets fed grapes? Actual Dad went around the green instead of going the straight way home but maybe he had to go the post office or something, except he drove right past it and kept going onto the highway, which we only go on when we're going to his house, but that wasn't supposed to be until Friday.

"Where are we going?" I asked, even though I knew I wasn't supposed to talk back right then.

"Home," he said, and then nothing again.

Turns out Actual Dad meant his home, which is its own home that's not an apartment. Where Actual Dad lives all the houses look pretty much the same because they're mobile homes, so you can pick them up and move them around with a truck. Since Actual Dad wasn't in a talking mood and who knows what I was doing there anyway, I decided to go to my room there and try to cast a spell, like maybe one to teleport me back to my real room where Melissa was. I closed my eyes and folded my legs underneath me and started to hum like Indian people do.

"Ohmmmmmmmmmmm," I said, and I went on for about thirty seconds and then I heard the doorknob turn, which made my heart leapfrog up into my throat because I thought maybe the spell was really working, but it turned out it was only Actual Dad. "Kevin?" he said, and he looked down at me and I don't know why, but he looked scared, like maybe something had happened to him when I was casting the spell.

"Huh?" I said.

"Get up off the floor," he said. "Sit down on the bed." He folded his arms and waited for me to get up, but he didn't look mad like he usually does when his arms are folded like that. I don't know why, but that scared me more because if he wasn't going to yell at me then what was he doing in here? So I got up and sat back down on the bed and looked at him but he didn't say anything, he just stared at the wall, which didn't even have any pictures or posters on it like my wall at home. My wall at home had posters of football players that I didn't even know who they were, but Old Dad put them up because he wants me to like football.

Finally he started talking but kept on looking at the wall. "This is where you're going to be staying from now on," he said. "It's for the best."

My stomach jiggled inside when he said it this time. He didn't look mean when he said it like he usually did, more like scared, and I've never seen Actual Dad look scared, even when our porch caught fire when Mom fell asleep on it with a cigarette back when we all lived together.

"But why?" I asked him. I don't really like Old Dad, and I don't really like the retards, but I like Mom and I like my room and I like living across from the river where the best bugs are.

"Your mom's got to take care of some stuff," he said.

"What stuff?" I said.

"Stuff," he said.

"WHAT STUFF?" I said in my acting-up voice. Usually I'm scared to use that around Actual Dad but this time I didn't care because I wanted to know, and I didn't care if I had to be a brat to find out.

"She's in some trouble, Kevin," and he said it louder because I asked him louder, but still he wasn't yelling or anything. I wanted to know what kind of trouble, because how do grown-ups even get in trouble?

"Your Mother's been doing some things she shouldn't have been doing. She's been putting you in danger and putting the retarded people in danger and the police found out about it and so they needed to put a stop to it. And you needed to be out of that house with that man who's also putting you in danger because he's a piece of shit and sorry, Kevin, your mother's pretty much a piece of shit, too."

"She's not a piece of shit," I said. "Don't say that just because she doesn't like you anymore."

"Oh, she's not a piece of shit?" he said. This time the loud was mad loud but still it didn't scare me because I was mad too, because he was talking about my mom and he shouldn't say stuff like that around me. That's what Dr. Imperioli said and he's a doctor, he should know. "*She* doesn't like *me*? Well you know what she does like, Kevin? Pot and Ritalin and my father's lawsuit. And that's about it."

He was lying because he was mad at my mom and his dad and that means there was nobody else for him, so why wouldn't he want me? But I was mad at him too and didn't care. I didn't want to live with him anymore. I wanted the neighbor's kids to fill up his whole house with sand from the parking lot and bury him like a hermit crab. But his hands were clenched up into balls like Old Dad's when he gets mad, and Mom wouldn't let him keep me forever anyway so I kept quiet. She'd grab onto me the next time I went home.

"I need to get Melissa," I said.

"We'll get your stuff tomorrow," he said. He didn't even ask who Melissa was. Sometimes it's like I'm not saying anything at all.

The next day I didn't say anything to Actual Dad from the time I woke up all the way through breakfast. He didn't try to talk to me either, even though he had no right to be mad at me. I didn't do anything to him except talk back but that was because he started it, and he said himself that it's not okay to start fights but it's okay to finish them. Finally he just said, "Hurry up with those Smacks," and I was glad to finally hear him say something but it wasn't an apology. It wasn't an "I'm sorry." All it meant was that it was time for me to go back home and get my stuff, but he'd be in for a surprise when Mom was there, and she would throw a fit and yell and she can really scream, Mom can. She'd get the neighbors over there and everything.

"Uh-huh," I said by accident. I meant to not talk to him at all that day.

But I did better on the truck ride over to Mom's. I didn't say a word and he played along. He didn't say a word either. He turned the radio on and it played some songs I know he liked, like "Walk This Way" and "Sweet Emotion," both by Aerosmith because it was Double Shot Thursday on WHCN. Actual Dad had the CD and listened to it a lot when he lived with us, but even then he never sang along like Mom did. Maybe he wasn't talking to her either, even all the way back then, and I just never noticed it because like Mom says, I can do the talking for a whole room full of people. Maybe I just talked right over them not talking to each other.

He didn't even talk when we pulled into the lot at Mom's house, even to say *stay in the truck*, which I was pretty sure he was going to say since I knew there was going to be some yelling going on. But he didn't tell me to get back in when I opened the truck door and jumped out and walked two steps behind him to the door. He didn't knock or anything when he got to it, just walked right in through it as if he lived there himself, even though Mom and Old Dad said he wasn't even welcome to come in when he dropped me off from the Y.

And then maybe Old Dad knew what game Actual Dad was playing because he looked right at him from the couch and he didn't say a word either. He just folded his arms and looked away, down to the ground instead of back at the TV. But Mom, she didn't play along. When she came out from her bedroom and saw Actual Dad standing there, she took in a gasp of air so big it was like she was going underwater and needed enough air to get her to the other side of the pool.

"You," she said. "Oh, you."

And then she came at him with her arms whirling around like a propeller, and she slapped him in the chest over and over again, even though Mom was always telling me and Jimmy not to hit. Not friends or enemies or anybody. But she kept slapping and slapping and she was crying as if she were the one being hurt instead of doing the hurting.

"In the *paper*," she yelled. "They're putting it in the *paper*."

Actual Dad let her thump her propeller arms all over him and he didn't even flinch. And I wished he would stop her because even if it didn't hurt I didn't want to watch it anymore. Even if it didn't hurt it wasn't right to hit like that. Even kids and retards know that.

"Mom," I said to her. "Mom, stop it."

But she didn't stop it, and she didn't say anything or even look over at me. All Actual Dad said was, "Kevin, get some stuff together."

When he said that then finally Mom did stop and fell to the floor, and she said, "What am I supposed to do now?" once, then twice, then over and over like a broken record. "What am I supposed to do now what am I supposed to do now what am I supposed to do now?"

I waited for her to crawl over to me and grab on to me, but she didn't even look over, even when I called out "Mom" again.

"Kevin, get your stuff now," Actual Dad said.

I ran into my room not because I wanted my stuff but just to get away. Just to see Melissa. Melissa was in there waiting for me. Waiting for a cricket, waiting for some fresh leaves, waiting for whatever praying mantises wait for. But I had nothing for her. No food, no nothing. How was I supposed to take care of her now? Actual Dad would probably let me keep her out in the open, which Mom wouldn't do, but all he had was that sandy little yard with nothing but the neighbor's kids and their stupid toy dump trucks. He didn't have the river or anything with all the spiders and moths and beetles.

"Melissa," I said.

She just sat rubbing her hands together as usual, waiting for whatever I was supposed to bring to her. I had nothing. I thought maybe I should run her back out to the river and put her on a leaf and let her do whatever she did before I found her. But she wouldn't like it out there anymore, not after living in a warm house where she didn't even have to look for her own food anymore. It wouldn't be right. I had nothing.

I had the kill jar.

"It's for the best, Melissa," I told her. She didn't understand. She wasn't human so she couldn't understand that. But I told her again anyway. "It's for the best."

She was just a bug. I told myself that. It was just me being stupid that I thought of her as anything else and gave her a name and everything. Melissa. Stupid Melissa. Stupid, stupid Kevin Jr.

But I kept saying "I'm sorry, Melissa" when I poured the nail polish remover onto the cotton balls in the kill jar. *I'm sorry, Melissa. I'm sorry, Melissa.* The nail polish was flower-scented instead of just regular-scented, but you could still smell the poison in it. Just flowers on top of the poison. I wondered if she'd smell it and think she was back home, back outside. Probably no. It was like the butterfly, just a stupid trick that couldn't fool anybody, even a stupid bug. A stupid bug like Melissa.

"I'm sorry, Melissa." I said it again when I scooped her up from the fishbowl and dropped her into the jar. I screwed the lid on and I held my breath so I could suffocate along with her, and we both held our breath, and I watched her until her little beggar arms twitched like a snapped rubber band, and then they stopped, and then the noise outside the room stopped too, and then my room just went away and the house just went away and then the roads outside and the river were all gone and everything everywhere in the whole world was gone. And I don't remember when I took my first breath again, but I must have because the whole world came back while I was lying there on the ground, and then I imagined what could've have happened while I was away.

Ramon Beats the Crap Out of George, a Man Half His Size

Ramon Aponte is Rumba Ramon in the New England Wrestling Association, and some of the other guys make fun of that but Adam used to tell him he moved like a dancer. And as a kid, his uncles too had told him he moved like a dancer, swaying down East Main, past Brass City Tattoo, where El Diablos inked a love even brighter than the chrome on their bikes, past the Iglesia Cristiana De La Familia that advertised Jesus on the same marquis that once advertised *The Godfather*, past the window where his mother watched him walk to the bus stop on the mornings he promised her he'd go all the way to school. And those kids at school, too, had told called him a dancer, a belly-dancer tap-dancer dance-line fag, until finally in eleventh grade he'd bled the words clean out of their mouths with knuckles he'd alchemied into brass.

So far, two miles is as far as he made it from that bus stop, those thugs. He could walk to every one of the hi-fi car stereo installation shops they all work at, but he never does. Because those two miles might as well be a million, because those kids don't know his name now only because they don't know anything, because someday when they do know his name he never wants to be close enough to hear them call it. But in the meantime he stays because Waterbury is cheap and only fifty miles from Stamford, from World Headquarters, where the contracts are made, where the rings aren't two-by-four platforms hammered by seventeen-year-old technical high school students who haven't juiced up enough yet to take a dive off the ropes themselves.

Now, still only two miles away from that bus stop, Ramon looks around his apartment, either room a perfect view from the other, not much to see no matter where he turns his head. But it's okay, because he doesn't want a home here.

Here is an extended-stay motel, a motor lodge. Someday, Rumba Ramon will have a nice place in Stamford, a townhouse just far enough from the MTA train tracks. But for now Ramon sits on brown velveteen, a couch retired from his mother's apartment, and stares at the one thing there that calls for attention: a seven-year-old girl doing a split on the wood floor.

"See, I told you I could do it," she says.

"I never said you couldn't," he says.

"Yeah, but I can."

He doesn't remember her name, something out there, Armenian or something. Lulu? Lala? She belongs to the lady on the first floor, has been coming to his door every afternoon for three months, since she spotted Adam moving boxes from Ramon's apartment to the bed of his baby-blue Ford Ranger.

"Where's your friend going?" she'd asked him.

"Don't know," Ramon answered.

"Can I come in?" she said.

"I guess," he said.

She, walked toward the corners of both the rooms and pressed her hands against the walls as if looking for the lever that would open up the secret passageway to where he really lived, because, man, obviously this was not a place to be. But no walls spun around behind the bookcase, there wasn't even a bookcase, so she finally folded herself cross-legged onto the heap of sheets in the bedroom.

"Where's your bed at?" she asked.

"Gone," he answered. "Where's your mother at?"

"Gone," she said.

Ramon has learned that seven-year-olds don't take hints any better than orders, so he lets her stay, do her splits and her head-stands, and sing "There Was an Old Lady Who Swallowed a Fly" because eventually she'll leave on her own. Like when her mother comes home from work, or like now, when George shuffles up to the second floor from the work shed he built for himself behind the parking lot. George owns the building, lives off the rent, and builds things he could never ever use, like rabbit pens and seesaws. He's been working on a houseboat that now sits on stilts in the patchy lot that is their backyard. He's ugly but friendly, his pants always cinched midway down his ass, which barely exists. He lets Ramon pay the rent whenever.

"Okay," the girl says from nowhere, and she sweeps her legs back together from the split. "Gotta go now." She kicks open the screen door and jumps down the porch stairs two at a time, some-how enough power in those steps to make the wood stairs crack beneath her forty-five pounds.

"Hello there, baby girl," George calls up from a flight below. "Lollipop."

Lahli. That's the girl's name.

He is an elephant in the ring. No style. No grace. He scares the ladies away, and they come to him, to dance with Rumba Ramon.

In the ring Ramon speaks in an accent he hasn't used since school, when all the second-generation Puerto Ricans pulled it out like a switchblade. He wears red trunks with a white star over the crotch, enters the ring in a ruffled tuxedo shirt that he tears off and throws at the nearest lady in the front row, a huge lady in a crowd of huge ladies with huge husbands and children with tits bigger than his mother's ever were.

"I brought something for you, Ramon." This is what Marty—tonight Lt. Mann—says, a pink tutu wadded up in the fist he holds high over his head. "Now do you want to dance or do you want to wrestle?"

The crowd in the Wallingford Industrial Complex should be bigger than the few dozen it is, Ramon thinks, but they were competing with the Greek Festival, and people around there only got one chance per year to get fat off of gyros and wedding cookies. And that crowd is bullshit because tonight Ramon is here to win, his first win in a couple months. Johnny, the promoter, arranged for it, a man who roots for the bad guys in the ring because it clarifies the distinction between good and evil, proves to the audience that good does not always triumph but the fight always goes on. That's what he told Ramon last time he came in for an oil change at the Quick Lube where Ramon works.

"See, people always love a great heel," he'd said. "Or hate them. Love to hate them. There wouldn't be a Jesus without a Judas."

Ramon doesn't know what that means. But it won't matter anyway, because the boos that will carry him backstage after his win will be as good as a lift above the shoulders, even if not as good as a gold belt around his waist.

The announcer steps into the ring and takes to the mic. "Ladies and gentlemen, are you ready? Tonight we have Rumba Ramon—"

And now Ramon grabs hold of Lt. Mann's arm and hammer-throws him into the ropes. It's before the bell, yes, but before the bell is right on time for this match. It's Rumba Ramon's job to cheat, and you better believe he's good enough for a title.

"Ladies and gentlemen, Rumba Ramon jumps the bell! Here is a man who will do anything to win."

He would do anything to win, if he could. But that's decided outside the ring, not here. So the referee retreats to the corner to allow Ramon to continue his fist-drop to Lt. Mann, who still lies diagonally across the mat.

They have planned some spots already in the locker room before the match. They decided on a quick start but that Ramon should quickly fade. The crowd will cheer Lt. Mann's triumph over Ramon, and Ramon's comeback will be fast, almost an accident, at the end of the match. Lt. Mann will be tired by then from thrashing Ramon early on, and the crowd will be pissed off before they have a chance to get bored.

So Ramon lets Marty pummel him for a few minutes, lets Marty's sweat drip from the bridge of his nose into Ramon's open eyes. By the time the ref signals to them to bring it home, Ramon's been pinned several times, each time barely writhing his way out from beneath Marty's arm. But now Ramon kicks back hard against Marty's chest, and Marty stumbles back two steps, stunned. Now Ramon hurls himself into the ropes and ricochets back with a high knee to Marty's ribs. Finally, it's time for Rumba Ramon's finisher, the Rumbero Shaker. Marty's chest heaves. He knows it's here, and as Ramon approaches, their eyes lock for one tiny moment.

Good match, those eyes say, because they won't say it out loud later.

Ramon bends down, hooks Marty's thighs onto his shoulders. The crowd hisses and yells and for a half minute that three dozen sounds like a whole arena, a whole goddamned packed arena, and it's easy, the Rumbero Shaker. Ramon begins a backward drop, and Marty falls like timber onto the mat, and Ramon drops his heavy chest against Marty's, and Marty is a good man, but no, son, Ramon is not sorry.

One.

Two.

Three!

"Fair and square?" the announces asks. "I don't know about that, ladies and gentlemen, but Rhumba Ramon is your winner here tonight!"

The scene barely registers to those fat families that come for the hot dogs because they never heard of souvlaki. But he will forever dance for them anyway. Because those boos will fade on his walk backstage, tonight the kitchenette of an abandoned car-accessories distributor, and by intermission those boos will have become Bic pens to autograph their photocopied programs. So he rhumbas his way down the aisles to the locker room, and in the crowd he notices

Lahli propped up above George's shoulders, and he quickly turns away because George is a nice enough guy and so what if he's with her too much, it's her mother should be paying attention to that shit. He turns back to the rest of the audience to take in the hate they throw at him, that call of Faggot coming from the left as he rhumbas down the line.

There was an old lady who swallowed a horse to swallow the goat to swallow the dog to swallow the cat to swallow the mouse to swallow the spider to swallow the fly. Lahli doesn't know why she swallowed the fly, perhaps she'll die.

This is what Ramon hears instead of Adam, who called Ramon—who has called Ramon—every Tuesday since he moved out. Ramon can barely hear Adam over Lahli's song, but he knows what he's saying:

"You've got to meet our little Chihuahua. I named him Rumba Rico. I don't know why, it just came out. It's funny, right, because you're so big and he's so small. But he totally thinks he's tough, you know, all three pounds of him. Maybe that's why I call him Rumba Rico—he's all tough on the outside, like a certain Rumba I know."

But Ramon can barely hear him say it. Adam said Ramon never really heard anything he ever said, anyway.

"God, Ramon, you never listen. Never. I'm just trying to be friends with you, okay? I don't want to just forget about you. What the hell is that singing?"

"Huh?" Ramon says. "Hey, I've got to get going."

Ramon listened plenty, though, before this call. Especially to this:

"I just need something that's going somewhere. This isn't going anywhere, you know? I gave up my own place for these two rooms because you promised it was just for a little while, and here we still are in two fucking rooms in Waterbury fucking Connecticut."

And to this:

"His name is Jarod. I'm so so so sorry, Ramon."

And to this:

"You know, Ramon, wrestling is not a job, okay? It's not a career. It's shouldn't even be a hobby for a twenty-nine-year-old man. It's just fucking make-believe fighting because you're too scared to fight for anything real. If you want to get beat up, do it for real outside Triangles like the rest of us faggots. Except being a faggot is the one thing you want to make believe you're not."

And as if Adam's spirit has lingered in the linoleum, crawled up through Lahli's bare feet, and spread through her blood like a hookworm, she stops singing and says:

"Why do you want to fight everybody?"

"It's not fighting," Ramon says. "It's wrestling."

"And you're so mean."

"I'm just mean, I guess," he says.

"No you're not. You're not mean now."

"Get the hell out of my house. Never come back, you stupid little shit."

Lahli stares back at him. "You're just faking."

Ramon crosses him arms. "I'm like the Incredible Hulk. When I'm mean I'm very, very mean. So don't make me be mean to you."

"How would I make you be mean to me?"

"Don't try."

Lahli pulls a backward somersault that rolls her all the way onto her feet. On the linoleum, with a spine that juts out from beneath a thin T-shirt three sizes too big for her, it must hurt. Ramon remembers seven, and that pain only comes if you think too much about the thing that hurt you.

"Why aren't you downstairs with George?" he says.

"'Cause Charlotte's home," she says, even though George's wife is a perfectly nice lady with a talking cockatoo that any seven-year-old of right mind and who's got shit else of her own should love.

"So?" he asks her.

"I don't want to," she says.

"Why not?"

Lahli sighs like Ramon is the dumbest cunt in the world, like Adam did when Ramon left for a match, or for training, or to kick a post out of the porch just because. Only Lahli understands *because* in a way Adam never did. "Because," she says. "Because because because."

"Alright," he says, since that's always been a good enough answer for him.

Ramon hates the drive to Stamford, an hour and ten on a good day, and there aren't any good days since no highway that went anywhere you'd want to be cuts through Waterbury. But today it's the worst, those roads to 95 stretch out forever like they're going to drop him off at the end of the world instead of Bridgeport, which is close to the end of the world anyway. And all these Buicks move too slow, and all these shut-down mills follow the riverbank like they're chasing him down Route 8, and he remembers the days when the Naugatuck River used to catch fire from whatever the mills dumped into it, and he wished like hell it would happen again. Let the river carry that fire like a fuse all the way back to Waterbury and detonate that shit. Let the whole city blow like a stick of dynamite.

Ramon's been booked down at headquarters. Johnny knows somebody who knows somebody who fucked somebody over and now owes him something, and Johnny—Johnny, Jesus bless his heart, pacemaker and all—called him up and told him that they needed some talent down in Stamford. "Yeah, some enhancement talent, you know, for the dark matches in between the real ones. It could be a chance to catch someone's eye, you know? Plus, a couple hundred bucks in your pocket, know what I mean?"

Of course Ramon knows what he means. He's not dumb. He means about $175 more than he'd take home after a day at the Quick Lube, and all he's gotta do for it is take a beating like he insulted someone's mother in front of a crowd that would jump the ropes and join in against him if they could. Exactly what he'd pray for at the Iglesia Cristiana De La Familia if Ramon was a praying man, which maybe he has been without even knowing it.

But the forever drive does end, and Ramon pulls into the parking lot for employees only, where the security guard asks for ID and matches the name to the one on their list. And the guard gives him clearance, and suddenly he's at the door, a door far away from any entrance he's ever used, not the door the regular rest of the world has to use. And then more security at the front desk, and then a name badge hung from his neck like he's somebody important, a doctor at a convention or a roadie.

Ramon walks from the marbled lobby into a hall that turns to tile, then carpet, then to rutted cement slabs layered with glossy latex paint, the same kind that shines off of any middle school locker room. But this room is not for school kids, and it's not for the executives and secretaries and middle managers. It's for talent. Talent like Ramon. Ramon wishes Adam could see him now. There's nothing fake about that name badge, nothing fake about his talent.

"Ramon Aponte. Hey, you talent?" some guy says.

"Yeah, I'm talent," he answers.

"I'm Dave. Talent too. You worked here before? You know the way around?"

"Nah, never been."

So Dave shows him the changing area, which Ramon doesn't need because he's already wearing plain red trunks beneath his warm-up suit. No costume tonight, because these guys don't want characters from the enhancement talent, just boring guys that the stars can bang around. And then on to the catering table, where Dave fills a plate with roast beef and potato salad and Ramon does the same, not hungry but wanting to accept anything they offer. Ramon finishes his plate but remembers nothing of the taste, and his stomach feels no fuller than it did a few minutes ago, when the stone pitted into his gut didn't have to share its space with anything.

"You want to check out the ring, warm up a little?" Dave asks, and Ramon shrugs, though of course he wants to check out the ring. Ramon knows that Dave must remember his first time back there, when he'd rather hold it in all night than ask where the bathroom is, when every man that walked past could turn him back into that fat ballet dancer at school if they wanted to. Ramon knows that he will remember it, every long second of what will be a very long night, and that one day he will act as if he has forgotten all of it too. One day when he no longer needs it.

But climbing up into the ring, he needs that now. Peeling off his warm-up suit, the first layer of sweat over his skin, his first run into the ropes and kick onto the mat—he needs all of that. Everything here is different. The ring is bigger. The ropes are real rope, not steel cable like the ones he whips his rivals into in the small time. The mat bounces him so high when he falls into it that he almost lands back up on his feet. But he will adjust. He will learn, and quickly, by throwing Dave too hard or too soft into the corner at first, by clotheslining too high, by rebounding too slowly from the mat slam he's taken.

"Alright, everybody out of the ring," somebody calls out, one of those assholes who don't need name badges because their importance is as good as monogrammed into their polo shirts. "Time to head backstage."

Ramon bends over to pull his warm-up suit back over his legs, and he shouldn't have eaten that roast beef because it's crawling back up his throat so hard that he's back at the catering table swallowing cupfuls of water just to keep it down. He takes a seat on a folding chair and real quick he's feeling better, almost good, almost alright as he watches the names walk by in their own warm-up suits. Deedee Shane, Michael "The Riptide" Mancini, The Corpsegrinder Crew, all walking by like it's nothing, not even thinking that he doesn't belong. And he's thinking then that he does, that this is where he needs to be, fifty miles from Ramon Aponte's home and square in the middle of Rumba Ramon's.

"Dave Allegrini?" another polo shirt calls out, and Ramon listens to Dave's nylon track pants chafe between his thighs, that swishing getting softer until Ramon can't hear anything, can just watch Dave's head nod up and down, up and down while the polo shirt talks straight into his clipboard. And then the polo shirt walks straight toward Ramon, and Ramon reaches down to his toes like he's stretching out his thighs, like whatever's on that clipboard doesn't mean shit to him.

"Ramon Aponte?" the guy says.

"Yeah?" Ramon answers.

"Alright, we're not going to be needing you to fight tonight. Got the dark matches filled up already. You can head on out whenever you want, just see the receptionist on your way out so you can fill the paperwork, get paid and everything. Thanks for coming down, sorry about the trip. We'll, uh, keep your name on our list, Ramon."

If he's not in the ring, Ramon wonders, why is he sweating? Why, if he's not in the ring, is his heart knocking against his chest like it's trying to bust out?

"Alright, man. Take care," Ramon says, because the man's holding out his hand like he's really going to walk away, and Ramon grabs on for a second too long, a little too hard, because yeah, that guy really is going to walk away.

The hammering has stopped. George has stepped off that goddamned houseboat long enough for Ramon to down a few Advil and plan out his farewell.

It's been real, George, but it's time for me to get out of here. Moving out toward Stamford, gonna get some better work down there. Any chance of using the deposit toward my last month, Georgie Boy?

So Ramon approaches the work shed, which he has never seen the inside of, and expects to find a sawhorse and tools and maybe even a cot or something, the amount of time he spends in there. He pushes open the door and there is a sawhorse, there are tools, and there is George and his dick squeezed tight in one hand, and there is Lahli with his other slid under her shorts, sprawled out over plywood like she's been taken down from the third ring, her eyes open and blinking, that same kind of stare he uses on the mat when he takes in everything with his eyes straight up to the ceiling, and Ramon knows exactly what she's looking for and that it's not up there, Lahli, so you can stop looking now, Lollipop.

"Oh," George says when he sees Ramon.

Ladies and gentlemen, even when the outcome is predetermined, there is a certain amount of belief that carries through every match. Like now, when George is juicing hardway, he believes that the houseboat might someday carry him downstream if only the river would flood enough for a current strong enough to push him out to sea. And Lahli, she believes it's her own blood she tracks in crosshatched prints across the gravel, and when she's inside she looks over and over for the cut and even though she can't find it, she knows it's there somewhere. And ladies and gentlemen, Ramon believes this most of all, because he's shooting this match, taking it over, fuck who's supposed to win and supposed to lose because this one is his to decide. He ain't the wrong one, he ain't the bad guy here, any audience could see if they would just care to look, which they never do, they never ever do. Rumba Ramon is your champion here tonight.

Mandatory Evacuations

The Filipino palm reader told my friend that she needed to wear jade on her pinkie to attract money. Then the palm reader said, You no find true love long time. My friend laughed at first, but then her boyfriend stopped calling, saying he was sick, down a week straight with body aches and laryngitis. He was lying, but it was true at least that he couldn't speak loud enough for me to make out any words when we ran into him at the R Bar on night seven. We walked in wearing mod dresses for the mod dance party happening later that night, and when he recognized her through the eyelashes and frosted lip gloss he blew her a kiss and bought us shots of Mandatory Evacuations, Katrina having made the Hurricane a drink locals no longer wanted to swallow. I was thinking, I shouldn't accept this, she's going to remember it as a nice thing he did for her and she'll think of that nice thing as evidence, now in support of and later against him. She was saying, he's a nice person, I don't think he'd do that to me, *that* being all the things we used to talk about over Bloody Marys and Denver omelets at the Athenian in Waterbury, back when we both lived there and didn't wish we didn't.

To distract my friend I told her about how en route to New Orleans I'd gotten an e-mail from a cousin: I have news about your father, if you are interested to know. If not, please disregard. It was signed, Sincerely. I am currently traveling, I responded, and wondered if that was the right thing to say. I'd never met my cousin, but I assumed English wasn't his first language, so everything would sound a little like it was meant for someone else. But it was obvious he didn't understand me at all if he offered only interested or not and expected one of them to be my answer.

My friend yelled, over Roger Daltrey, over "My Generation": Christ, can't some bitches just go out and d-d-d-dance?

On the way back to her apartment, we stopped for beignets, so much powdered sugar ashing onto the truck's bench seat that it looked like we'd driven with the windows down through a fire. The next morning we took turns trying to feel better in the bathroom, but the bathroom was hotter than the dance floor. I sweated even in the shower, and it felt like being ganged up on.

Afterward I dried out in air-conditioning and read in an e-mail that my father had been buried in Houston the week before. I wrote back asking why Houston, because as far as I knew it was a place my father had never been, but I asked it fully aware that as far as my father had known, I'd never been to New Orleans. It all just went to show. Then my friend said, from the other room: He called. He dumped me. I thought: You no find true love long time, and wondered how the Filipino palm reader expected money for offering a fortune like that, when I wouldn't dare even say it aloud. Then I realized that that was it exactly. That was exactly it.

Flipping Property

1. What is preforeclosure, and how can you make it work to your advantage? In the next half hour, world-renowned real-estate guru Truman Evans will show you with his patented No Money Down Deal-Sealer's System.

The way I understood it was like this: most people hoard more than they'll ever need in this life like it's going to give them a head start in the next one. You know, the two-for-one, the family size, the value size, the free six-inch sub with the purchase of a footlong and medium soda IN-STORE ONLY COUPON MUST BE PRESENTED AT TIME OF ORDER, the six-CD stereo upgrade for a limited time only with a forty-eight-month lease at your friendly neighborhood Ford dealer NOT ALL LESSEES WILL QUALIFY, the Unlimited Nights and Weekends Families Talk for Free plan WITH THE PURCHASE OF FOUR (4) V600 CAMERA PHONES, the three-thousand-dollar Home Depot gift card WITH YOUR DOWN PAYMENT ON A NEW PREFABRICATED HOME AT GARDENIA GARDENS MINIMUM 1800SQ PLAN WITH FINANCING THROUGH FIRST UNITED BANK MEMBER FDIC, the people die every day doesn't your family deserve more coverage YOU AUTOMATICALLY QUALIFY IF YOU'RE A NON-SMOKER, etc. and so forth.

But some people can't even keep their hands on the barest needs. Terrell Berm, for example, barely keeping the roof over his pock-marked little head after the divorce and the bankruptcy and probably a stint or two at the Who Owns You Now rehab facility down on West Main. I didn't know Terrell Berm from any of the other guys living in any of the other gutted-out modular homes up and down the gutted-out modular streets down in the Valley, but I knew the type. I figured someone like Terrell Berm would want to be rid of his preforeclosed property, his preforeclosed goddamned life, so bad he'd pay the closing cost and send me a greeting card in the mail afterward. That's why I was feeling alright when I pulled the Tempo over and slipped that envelope into Mr. Terrell Berm's mailbox. Inside was the Magnetic Marketing Letter I'd printed up on the Deskjet at work: *I buy houses in any condition! Quick closings! Turn your undesirable property into DESIRABLE CASH!!!* Everything was red and blue on white, because cash is American is good. That's what Truman Evans said, to identify yourself with something positive, something that doesn't say, *You poor, losing bastard, I will take from you the last thing in this life that is yours.* A nicotine-beige curtain fluttered but I missed the face behind it. Enjoy your magnet, Mr. Terrell Berm, I thought. Seal your bills to the refrigerator with it or, if the bills don't make it that far, the Chinese takeout menu or a coupon for a dollar off two rolls of Pillsbury biscuits. Just maybe pause a minute at the name in red caps: LIZA BUSHKA, your friend in finance, or just CASH!!!—whatever's prettier.

Mr. Terrell Berm owned, or at least used to pay the mortgage on, a double-wide in Naugatuck set just down a ways from that business park filled with empty warehouses which every once in a while hosts a traveling discount-book sale. I knew that because I work at the bank that owns his remortgaged mortgage, dialing the phone numbers that the recordings are sorry are no longer in service, licking the envelopes for those preforeclosure letters that go straight into the trash. 99 N. N St. More like a stutter than an address, or a candy bar you'd buy at the Dollar Value—like, the N&Ns right next to the Snuckers and Three Nougateers, that chocolate that's so cheap your mouth ulcers if you eat it. Even my kids don't beg for that crap. That's what the house was too, a knock-off of a home, an ugly 2/1 in a puke-green color that's only used for cheap siding and Tupperware. And that was the only green there. It's funny—you think grass is free, I mean it's everywhere, some states and countries are nothing but grass, people mow it down for Crissakes, but some poor bastards just can't get any to grow in their forty-by-fifty lots. It's like some kind of scarlet letter, only shit brown. The kind of shit-brown yard with a busted bicycle plopped right in the middle like the topper on an ugly birthday cake.

The Magnetic Marketing Letter didn't list my address two exits further down Route 8: 97 Harpers Ferry Road in Waterbury, the city that people in Naugatuck use to remind them that things could be worse. Terrell Berm didn't need to know that I don't even have the down payment for a house of my own yet. Real estate negotiation is all in presentation, in confidence, and he didn't need to know I don't have that either. Because according to Truman Evans's patented No Money Down Deal-Sealer's System, you don't really need money to make money. You just need a little creative self-marketing, a hard-money loan, and some carpeting to slap into a distressed property before you sell it, flip it, for market value without a single mortgage payment due. So I pulled away from the house with my sunglasses on because I thought maybe things were changing. Maybe I could be someone who could wear sunglasses without feeling like a jerk.

True, Truman Evans's No Money Down Deal-Sealer's System didn't include a chapter on how to make your kids' feet stop growing long enough for you to buy the decorative Ficuses you can't even afford for your own home, or how to live off the life-insurance policy your dead husband would've left behind if you hadn't insisted there wasn't any point in getting married, or how to stop Caleb's night terrors that set him off screaming at least three times a night and start Jenna crying right along with him when—Jesus, your head—this is the only time you get to study the No Money Down Deal-Sealer's System so can't you just be a big boy and sleep through one freaking night. I'm not stupid, I could see the holes. But the infomercial had offered a thirty-day introductory trial of the entire system for just the cost of shipping and handling, and then they'd asked, *What do you have to lose?* Right up until then I'd been laughing at all the fools in the commercial, their stiff hair blowing in one Dippity-Do as they were interviewed in front of their new motorboats, but that question brought me right back down. What do you have to lose, Liza? I tell you, I thought a long time about that question, and to this day I haven't come up with an answer.

2. Truman Evans first began investing in preforeclosures as a penniless undergraduate at the University of Illinois. By the time he earned his degree, he'd already made his first million. Now, Truman will show you how to take control of your own lives, your finances, your destinies, with his patented No Money Down Deal-Sealer's System and optional seminars.

I was nineteen. I wanted a dog but the complex we were living in wouldn't allow them, and even if they did Scotty wouldn't. "I don't want to share you with a dog," he'd say. So I'd visit pounds and shelters with a bundle of Milkbones wrapped up in my pocket and slip them between the wires on the cages. I'm sorry I can't take you home, I'd tell them, but I'm sure you'll find a fine one eventually.

I also wanted cancer. Not to die from it, but to survive it. Any idiot with the money for tuition could get a degree, but to beat malignancy and hardly even miss a day at the call center—that was something worth trying. So I took up smoking and tanning and eventually went to Dr. Sizemore with my symptoms: fatigue, nightsweats, nausea, constipation.

"Well, you've got great iron in your blood," Dr. Sizemore told me. "I'd say you're feeling exactly how you're supposed to be feeling." He flipped through the chart, then looked up at me funny like there was grape jelly crusted all over my face. "You do know you're pregnant, don't you?"

"Um, I guess so," I answered. And the sickness hit hard right then, and all at once I had to puke and pee, and who was going to buy the formula and diapers and Diaper Genies and the little outfits with little pink gingham ruffles on the ass? But it was like drinking too much—after I threw up into the trash can I didn't feel so bad anymore. I still wanted a dog, but I knew Scotty would at least agree to a baby since he was one of twelve himself. That kind of stuff just made sense to him. A baby seemed less like sharing me than getting more of me, only thinking that made me sick all over again. Goddamned hormones.

I told my mother first. "Ah, crap," she said. "You know you don't have to marry him."

"I know," I answered.

Then I told Scotty. "How about that," he said. "You know we have to get married."

"I know," I answered.

Scotty came home the next day with a quarter-carat ring and a pair of tiny white booties. My mother didn't counteroffer, so I took the ring and strung it onto a gold-plated chain, since it was too small even for my pinky, and I wore it for special occasions like pig roasts and wakes. It was pretty and all, don't get me wrong, but I don't know who it was he was thinking of when he bought something that tiny. Maybe it was for his first girlfriend, the tiny Puerto Rican he brought to junior prom, or maybe he was just trying wish me into something easier to manage.

3. With the help of Truman Evans's patented No Money Down Deal-Sealer's System, you'll learn how to hone in on sellers who aren't even aware that their properties are on the market! In the end, your sellers will be thanking you for saving their ravaged credit, and your bank account will be thanking them for the fat profits!

Mom smeared some more peanut butter on the toast she eats for dinner every night.

"You're wasting your money on that, you know," she said.

I'd spread out two days' worth of newspapers and three months' worth of junk mail to camouflage the Deal-Sealer's binder, although really, I knew better.

"I'm not wasting any money except $9.99 shipping and handling," I told her. "It's a thirty-day trail and I'm sending it back after I finish it."

"You spent $9.99 on that?" she asked, like it was even worse than she expected.

In the pauses between the thumps and screams coming from the living room, the characters in a mind-murdering cartoon chanted a chorus to a song that gets stuck in my head for days, a whole string of gibberish that means nothing except that an overpaid Disney songwriter was too lazy to think of actual words. Someone probably earned six figures for that song, and yeah, I spent ten dollars on a white binder that was supposed to tell me how to buy a house even I wouldn't live in, and maybe, by some act of God and legal fine print, I might've made a thousand dollars profit so I could invest in my next slum. And yeah, maybe I did have a better chance of writing one of those Disney songs than making this thing work, but I had three days left with the system and damned if I wasn't going to try and make at least the $9.99 back.

Mom pushed the toast crumbs over the edge of the table and onto the floor. "I'll sweep tomorrow," she said. "I have to get to work. Jenna had a little bit of a fever today so you might want to put her to bed early. And Caleb's probably going to catch it so you might as well put him to bed too."

I nodded. I guess the fever didn't weaken their pile-driving muscles, but hey, I planned on putting them to bed early anyway, get in some good study time on my last three nights with that binder. I scanned Tuesday's paper while Mom gathered up her work smock and pocketbook, which seemed to take about ten minutes if I were counting.

Finally she mumbled goodnight, and I pulled out the Deal-Sealer's System before the door closed all the way behind her. I had some work to do. See, Truman Evans said the Magnetic Marketing Letters just plant an idea in, say, a Terrell Berm's head. Selling them on the idea was up to us. So I opened up to page 73, to the script Truman Evans gave us to follow, more or less, when contacting a potential seller. The script didn't call for a five- and three-year-old, so I walked into the living room.

"Hey, guys," I said, "we're going to play a game. You guys get to be really, really quiet while I'm on the phone. Whoever's quiet the whole time gets a Toaster Strudel."

Caleb rolled off the couch right on top of Jenna. "We hate this game, Mom," and like usual Jenna followed up with, "Yeah."

"Well, it can be a game and you get a Toaster Strudel or it can be an order and you get a swift kick in the butt. Your choice."

I walked away there because they might actually have considered it a choice, and whichever one they went with there was still only maybe a 30/70 chance of ten minutes of quiet. I picked up the phone and dialed the number I wrote on one of the pieces of junk mail, a credit card offer that was obviously an oversight in their credit-check process or else a downright taunt. The line rang and I stared down into the script, wishing I'd memorized it like I memorized the role of Rizzo that I didn't get in my high school's production of *Grease*. It was on three rings, four, then finally,

"Uhnn?" a voice on the other end said. I recognized that voice, a Pall Mall and Crystal Light voice.

"Yes, hello? Is Mr. Terrell Berm available?"

"Who's this?" he said.

"Hi, I'm Liza Bushka. I'm an independent real-estate investor and I'm interested in talking to you about your real-estate house or property located at 99 N. N St."

"What about it?" he said.

"Well, I understand that you've had some trouble making payments lately, and I'm prepared to offer what I hope is a solution that—"

"Are you from the bank?" he asked.

"Um, no, not really," I said.

"Then what the hell are you calling about?"

"It's ... I'm interested in perhaps talking to you about potentially purchasing your home for a fair and reasonable—"

"You got the wrong number, lady. My house isn't for sale."

"Well, I understand that it isn't currently on the market, but I was hoping perhaps that we might discuss the possibility of possibly considering a sale, which would," I checked the script, "perhaps circumvent the possibility of foreclosure that you are now currently facing."

"What in the hell are you talking about? This house isn't for sale," he said.

"Yes, I understand that it isn't *now* for sale," I said.

"It isn't ever for sale. What in the hell are you talking about?" He choked out a courser voice. "Where the hell do you think I'm going to live? Are you that magnet?"

"Um, well," I said. It might as well have been *Grease* in front of me by then. "By clearing the burden of a mortgage, you could possibly find another—"

"No, lady, you possibly find yourself another shithead to steal a house from." He was screaming then, and let me tell you that voice didn't sound any prettier the louder it blew. "You want to take away a man's home? What do you even know about a home? You're probably some kind of dyke, right, don't want a man to have a home of his own?"

"Um, no, I'm not a dyke, I'm an independent real-estate—"

"If you're not a dyke you're a slut. I bet you're a whore and a whore needs a whorehouse, don't she."

I hung up the phone and shook a couple of Toaster Strudels from their box in the freezer. "You guys were good," I called out to Caleb and Jenna, though I guess not loud enough for them to hear.

---

4. You might be asking by now if flipping is legal and if you can do it with no cash or credit. The answers are yes and yes!

I admit that Scotty was good. He worked hard, I mean legendary hard, down at Browman Bros., so hard that they broke the rules and put him on the concrete pumps at full union scale within six months of his starting there. I can tell you that because Mr. Browman and everybody at the company still tell me that if I run into one of them at PathMark, and it's like they're trying to convince me to think good of him when they see my carriage full of PathMark Peanut Butter and PathMark Tuna Fish and PathMark Everything instead of Name Brand Anything. But I know he worked hard. Seventeen dollars an hour on site days, plenty of time and a half. By the time Jenna came two years after Caleb we had the health insurance to pay for her to be born. I just worked part-time at the florist, which smelled nice and wasn't so bad, really.

And he was a good father. Our kids had nice clothes and nice toys. "Too many toys," my mother said. "You never had that many toys," as if that means something, as if I'm what I want my kids to grow up to be. The man was down on his knees every night building Lincoln Log cabins with them before he even took his boots off. That's what made hating him so hard. The World's Greatest Dad cap me and the kids gave him last Father's Day, that wasn't just a cheap novelty. He could've won that contest. But when he got me the matching Mom cap, I thought it was a practical joke. Because, really, I was still thinking about that dog. Dry food in a bowl, some newspapers on the floor, a rubber bone and a tie outside—that I could handle. But watching Scotty watch *Pocahontas* for the eighteenth time that week with Caleb and Jenna made me want to walk out into the winter, leave a trail of footprints to the Mad River that'd be long snowed over by the time anyone realized I was gone.

Instead I told Scotty that I wanted to take some classes at Mattatuck Community College.

"You're going to drive all the way across town every day, and all the way back, probably quit your job that you barely work at as it is, suck up half my paycheck into tuition and half dumping the kids into daycare, so that you can 'better yourself'? Better your kids, babe," he said.

Then I told him I wanted to take karate, get strong, get out of the house a couple of nights a week.

"Karate? You? Babe, you cry when you stub your toe. You never even did that Tai Bo video I got you last year."

Then I told him I wanted to leave him.

"Liza, you can't." He said it once, twice, over and over again, and his voice broke down like a truck, and the tears fell so hard I swear they stripped his face away, and I saw past his flesh to the chasm right in the center of him, and I knew what he said was right. Liza, you can't. Because maybe the kind of need we had for each other was like drowning people who pull the other one down and ride them like a raft to shore, but it was need nonetheless.

5. Truman Evans's course details his exclusive step-by-step process for revitalizing distressed properties. Turn real-estate lemons into lemonade with the No Money Down Deal-Sealer's System!

Truman Evans sold my name to about a thousand mailing lists, the son of a bitch.

"I told you that was a waste of money," Mom said. "And a waste of time."

"You never said it was a waste of time," I said, but really I just called her on a technicality since waste of time is pretty much built into everything I do.

Used car ad. Another credit card offer. Sewage bill. Electric bill. Letter.

But not really. No stamp, no address, just Liza Bushka printed in block letters like Caleb uses. I don't know if you understand this, but people like me don't get letters. If I was an army wife, I wouldn't get letters. Even the Austrian pen pal I wrote to in the fifth grade never wrote one back. So I didn't need to know what was inside to know what was inside, but I opened it anyway because it was that or the electric bill.

The magnet tumbled out when I unfolded the page, a red-ink scrawl on lined Highland Manufacturing memo paper.

Dear Liza,

I don't want your whore magnat. Your not getting my house and neither is anybody. Your a whore and that's why your man didn't marry you.

From,

Terrell Berm

"Jesus Christ," I yelled, and I wanted forceful but it came out wobbly instead. "Crazy son of a bitch, Jesus Christ." I hopped up and locked the doors even though I didn't want to be near them, and I didn't want to walk past the windows with that crazy son of a bitch a few miles away or maybe right outside, who the hell even knew.

"Caleb and Jenna, come in here," I called, even though I don't know why they needed to be in there or what I was going to tell them.

"What's your problem?" Mom asked, still smearing that peanut butter on her toast.

"*This* is my problem," and I showed her the letter.

She read it over and handed it back to me. "Well what do you expect, going around trying to buy houses you can't afford from people who can't afford to give one up?"

"I don't expect to be stalked," I said.

"What do you want?" Caleb said, Jenna trailing right behind him like his security blanket.

"Nothing. Just play in here for a little bit, okay?"

"But you never let us play in the kitchen," he said.

"Yeah, well, happy birthday."

"It's not my birfday," Jenna said, but Caleb, he got it even though he shouldn't have, and he glared right into me.

Mom started back up. "You're not being stalked, you're being put back in your place. It's insulting to people, acting like you're better than them. Plus, why're you giving out our address?"

"Hello, the phonebook, the goddamned *newspaper* printed my personal business all over this goddamned town, remember?

Freaking hell, I'm just trying to act better than *I* am. What the hell am I supposed to do, live in this hole forever? Lick envelopes forever? I mean," and it came out too quick, "don't you ever regret having me so young?"

She thought for a minute. "Nah. I wasn't doing anything better with myself. I mean, could you imagine life without these guys?"

Sometimes I cry thinking that this woman will someday die, and that the last thing that makes sense on this earth will die with her. Why couldn't I have inherited that sense, that pure logic that no science or religion could possibly stand up against, instead of these freckles on my shoulders? See, life without them goes like this:

I went through Mattatuck, got licensed as an LPN, and signed up with one of those traveling nursing agencies that sends me to Arizona or New Mexico or I don't know, just someplace warm, Hawaii even. Or I stayed on singing in that band I joined for three weeks in high school, and we're not famous or anything, but we do weddings and high school reunions, the occasional county fair. Or I'm really fit, a runner, a cyclist.

But the Department of Children and Families listens in outside triplexes, waiting for the chance to swoop down and prove you don't love your babies, so I just said, "Nope."

But it still scares me, sometimes, to look at my children. Jenna is so pretty that I want to take her to the doctor to fix it. There's no good to come out of that kind of pretty. And Caleb—Caleb is the kind of smart they call precocious but I call unnerving. He was looking at me there in the kitchen, and I knew he knew that I make everything up on the spot. And I could only look back at him and think, *Where did I come up with a name like Caleb?*

6. Truman Evans's No Money Down Deal-Sealer's System isn't the cheapest real-estate course out there, but then again, the best never comes cheap.

What you need to know, what Terrell Berm and everybody needs to know, is that Scotty isn't better off. No way, no heaven in any religion could match what he wanted on earth. Caleb and Jenna sure as hell aren't better off. I'm not even better off. Maybe I wouldn't get that ring resized, maybe I told him once or twice that it was because I had to get out there and live some first, but I know now it was just to hear him say, *Liza, you can't.* Liza, you can't leave. Liza, you can't possibly understand how deep you're in. You can't love them alone the way that I can.

And it was his love that killed him, so big it just popped him right open. Except he got a little help from a die-cast fire truck and some cement basement stairs. Since we were on the first floor we were lucky enough to get use of the cellar, which meant more room for more stuff we didn't really need. And listen, I was always telling Caleb not to leave that stuff around the house like that, and I was always telling Scotty to back me up on it. They never listened, never. So when me and the kids came home one day and the door to the cellar was open outside and we couldn't find Daddy anywhere, even with all of us calling out for ten minutes, I knew I should've sent them to their rooms before I did anything else, but I was scared. And I don't know what they saw when I pulled the door open wide, but I saw first the dollhouse half-finished, and I thought you fool, you stupid goddamned idiot, why was the one you bought for Jenna a year ago not good enough? But when I dropped down to my knees and put his head on my lap and soaked up that blood on his hair, that blood that sank into my own skin and colored it for days, I understood finally the kind of love that Scotty felt, and I understood that I'd never feel it, and I told him Scotty, Scotty, I wish I could, Scotty.

7. If at any point within the thirty-day trial period you're unsatisfied with Truman Evans's Deal-Sealer's System, simply return it no questions asked. Sorry, shipping and handling nonrefundable.

Mom was on her way out the door when the phone rang.

"I got a dick you can suck if you need the money," Terrell Berm said.

I pulled a big stream of air into my lungs so I could yell, but suddenly I was crying instead, crying, which I hadn't done in three months, and that bastard made me remember it, and he could die himself for that. "Go to hell, you motherfucker," I said.

"What's the matter, whore? Don't you want my property no more?"

"I don't care about the fucking property," I screamed into the phone, then hung up, and then whipped the receiver across the room into the cereal cabinet. Then Jenna was crying, and Caleb looked up at me with the kind of disappointed eyes that no five-year-old should have earned yet.

"Mommy," he said.

"She meant 'flipping property,' Caleb," my mother said.

"No I didn't," I said. "Mommy's mad and she shouldn't say things like that around you but that's how mad she is. She's sorry you had to hear it, but sometimes life just isn't good and she's sorry you have to hear that too."

Caleb stared up with those caramel eyes that came straight from his father, a whole face that came straight from his father, and I wished I could have seen right through to his insides so I'd know where they came from, if there was any chance at all, because my children, oh my children I am sorry.

Nadja Rides the Bear

His mother called him Samuel, but by his second day in Pony he knew enough to go by Sam. His second day in Pony was thirty-seven years before, when he was four, and his last day was Thursday, when he stopped in for a Mountain Dew and to grab a roll of TP out of the men's room at the Citgo.

He'd run into his father by the Big Grab display on the way out.

"Shalom," his father said when he saw Sam.

"How," Sam said.

It was the setup to a joke they never figured out a punchline for: an Indian and a Jew walk into a bar. They hadn't told it since the last time that literally happened, when the two of them walked into Stacey's up in the Gallatin Gateway. That was the night some nineteen-year-old rancher cold-cocked Sam after Sam bought a Nuts and Berries with a Kokanee chaser for the rancher's new child bride. Sam couldn't blame himself for trying; puberty for that girl had been like a cancer, normal cell division that forgot to shut itself off. Sam knew as he put his money on the bar that his chance of getting into a fight was so high it wasn't even chance and his chance of getting laid was snake-eyes, but at least some contact was guaranteed, this at a time when he sometimes forgot he carried with him his own body. Sam's father had slept with his head on the bar through the brawl and for another hour afterward, when the bartender helped Sam throw him into the hatchback of his own Plymouth Horizon.

Nowadays they were selling logoed ringer tees and ball caps to Montana State students at Stacey's. The whole place had changed a lot. The old-timers in these parts always complained about that, these goddamn *nowadays*, but as far as Sam could tell, nothing changing sucked just as bad.

His father was staring at the Combos. "They got any of them peanut butter ones that you can see?" he asked.

Sam's hand was shoved tight in his pocket, the sweat of his palm moistening a dollar so that it could rip in half without a sound, as if the damn thing wasn't useless enough as it was.

He said, "Don't think they make those anymore. It's all just pizza or nacho cheddar."

His father hooked a thumb around his belt loop, a morsel of bone and flesh so hearty the waist of his britches sunk low enough for a bit of his shirt to untuck. The shirt was missing a button, and through the gap Sam could see flesh, and Sam found it hard to turn away.

"Well, ain't that a bitch," Sam's father said. "Guess I'll be seeing you around, then."

"Yessir," Sam said. He figured the old bear would die before that ever happened, but then again, he'd thought the same thing the last time he saw the guy thirteen years before.

Nadja watched a moose nose through a pile of damp brush that she and Chris had collected that day. Nadja was sleeping in the truck because she told Chris she was on her period, which she'd only said because she didn't want to have sex and knew that Chris wouldn't want a stain on his minus-twenty-degree-rated Marmot mummy bag. Chris had told her that bears could smell menstrual blood and that she shouldn't sleep in the tent at all. Later she'd learned that sex wouldn't have been allowed anyway because bears could smell that too, so the whole lie was a waste of time, which was what her mother used to say every lie turned out to be.

"Oh, moose," she whispered. "Ca-ca." She didn't know if she should be making noise or keeping quiet, so she decided on making noise only she could hear. That way she couldn't really be accused of anything. Even the mosquito on her cheek didn't flutter, though, so she laid back down and shut her eyes tight.

Over the next hours, the space between the trees turned from navy to indigo to seafoam blue, a tropical drink watering down with melted ice. Nadja thought about the Mai Tai she'd had at some warehouse-sized Chinese place in Bozeman right before they came to Potosi. It came in a plastic cup shaped like a coconut and tasted like the flavor of freezer pop that she and her sister used to leave untouched until the rest of the better flavors were gone. She remembered they didn't come in flavors, they came in colors. Red, orange, yellow. The Mai Tai was blue. The blue freezer pops left her tongue that color and let the world know that they were paid for with food stamps.

Then she fell asleep and dreamt that she was drinking blue water, quarts and quarts of it. Her mouth was dry as a scab when Chris lunged inside the bed of the truck.

"A fucking bear," Chris said.

"What?" Nadja said.

"There was a bear outside my tent. Didn't you hear the bear?"

"I don't know," she said. "Are you sure it was a bear?"

"Yes, I'm sure it was a bear. They don't make raccoons bigger than my tent. It was out there for like an hour. Didn't you hear anything?"

"No," Nadja said. "Are you sure it wasn't a moose?"

"It wasn't a moose. The damn thing could've got me." He dropped his head into his hands like he'd given something up, but she knew he'd actually earned something: the right to say he'd survived a grizzly attack. "Man, I'm glad you were in the truck," he said, as if it were he who'd tucked her safely in there instead of her own dishonesty.

"Yeah," she said. "Me too."

It was early in the season still, midweek, time for Sam to catch up on his paperwork. But there were people around already. Last night there was the sound of a truck bumping over the washboard dirt, and through the trees from his site he could make out a two-person Kelty in a shade of blue that wouldn't be camouflaged on a Caribbean beach. After that it was mostly quiet, quiet enough to hear the crackle of a campfire but still he couldn't make out the voices. One was too deep, the other too soft.

The truck was four-cylinders short of the kind a militia crew would roll in on and too well-tuned to be driven by some meth-heads run out of Bozeman by their long-suffering mothers or no-more-chances dealers.

Maybe they were on the trail of his father, Rudy Rides the Bear, for debts unpaid.

They were here for the hot springs. The Kelty said it all.

A breeze seeped through the cracks of Sam's trailer, and still the walls sweated with the residue of his breath, which he couldn't ever keep from being hot.

Potosi was in Bureau of Land Management forest just down the way from Pony. You could drive right up to camp and still feel like you'd done something remarkable because even the tire treads left behind by the last Ford Ranger seemed somehow ancient. A hot spring sat about half a mile in, and since it was BLM land you could go nude by law. It was the government's way of saying, go ahead, be naked on our dime. Really all we ever wanted was to fuck you. They'd even built a wooden fence around the hot spring so you couldn't miss it, even though everybody did. Anyone one thousand feet up the trail was looking for the water they hadn't heard rushing since twelve hundred feet back.

Chris made it farther up the wrong way long before Nadja did, and by the time she found him, he was holding a gun that wasn't his in the hand he didn't favor, as if he'd changed into a different man altogether in the time it took for her to walk fifty yards uphill. He was standing beside a man whom at first Nadja took for a ghost because she didn't think it was possible for living souls to overlap in that much land, one of the only reasons she'd agreed to go on this trip with Chris in the first place.

"Hey," Chris said. "This is Sam."

Sam was six-foot-four at least and only a fraction of it was torso. He tipped his hat at her, index finger and thumb kissing at the brim, his other fingers splayed like peacock feathers. If they hadn't been under a canopy of pines already, it would've made for a hell of a shadow puppet.

"Howdy," he said.

Even after he dropped his hand from his hat back down to his waist, Nadja dwelled on Sam's fingers, the longest she'd ever seen on a man, adapted to some purpose that only native Montanans would have known about. They must've been a tool you needed in a place where "cowboy" was a job and not a cut of denim. Sam didn't wear denim. He wore the standard-issue mud brown of a ranger, his bark-colored skin just a few shades off from his trousers. He was ugly in any quantitative sense. But he was elegant in some way. Nadja had not thought of the word *elegant* since her mother made her model for no real occasion one sequined monstrosity after another at Denise's Bridal Affair, pretending her daughter was a pageanteer and hadn't maxed out at a B-cup. Her mother would've filled out pageant gowns in her day, had there been sequins in Korçë instead of communist beige, but even on her mother it would not have been truly elegant. It was a difficult quality to come by. An unexpected thing to find in the woods.

"Chris here was just telling me about your bear," Sam said.

"Oh," Nadja said. "The bear." Sam's fingers were villainous in addition to elegant. She recalled a childhood bad guy, a Purple Pie Eater.

She turned to Chris. He was holding the gun away from his body. It was a responsibility he obviously didn't want, like a bag of dog shit collected after a walk. His fingers were knobby around the knuckle and soft at the pads. But he was smiling, laughing even, squinting in the full shadow of the trees. He'd eaten elk back in Bozeman, breaking nine years of vegetarianism, and he was pushing full steam ahead. Wildness, at best, was adorable on him.

"Sam said grizzlies are out like crazy now," Chris said. "A mother with a couple of yearlings has been hanging around the site. It could've been her. The mothers are the most dangerous too. Crazy, right? Outside of our tent?"

"Crazy," Nadja said. She felt the brim of Sam's ranger hat still pointed in her direction, so she turned behind her to look at the valley.

"Don't worry, bears ain't really in love with humans," Sam said. "They're in love with what you're cooking, mostly."

"He said bear spray doesn't work," Chris said. "Glorified pepper spray."

Sam tapped a canister of it that poked out of a holster in his belt. "Nah, I said it might work. Might not. Depends on the wind, depends on the bear, depends on how good your aim is when you're shaking so bad you'd need all four of your arms to hold the can steady. Anyway, it's better than nothing."

"But not as good as this," Chris said. He meant the gun but he didn't look at it. On Chris the steel looked like jewelry. Nadja hated jewelry on men, the Eastern European thuggery of it, the gold rings of her father. Even as a child she suspected it was tasteless, those gold rings and hidden fifties stuffed into the pockets of Kangaroos sneakers.

"A gun is better than the spray," Sam said. "It's not good. Probably it's not ever right to look at a gun and call it a good thing."

Nadja finally looked back at Sam, his braid snaking down his back and his missing tooth and the golden Star of David resting on a cloud of white chest hair. He took the gun back from Chris and placed it back in its holster, and suddenly it all seemed like nature again. Nature was all around: animals stalking them, water warmed by violent geothermic rumblings just beneath the crust of the earth. Every terrifying thing back in its place.

Later Sam watched Nadja and Chris at the hot spring. They sat not across from each other and not next to each other, either. They sat in a semicircle, if two people could make such a thing. As if waiting for other people to fill in the spaces.

"Shalom," Sam's father said. He pulled from a can of Kokanee and sat on a case of it in front of the Airstream Sam had left parked there so long it seemed a geologic feature.

"Citgo guys point you out here?" Sam asked.

"I smelled you on the wind," he said.

"I'm having company," Sam said.

"I'm good company." Sam noticed his father's right hip sat lower than his left. One side of the case near gone.

"A lady," Sam said.

"A lady with a fella. I saw them at their pickup truck."

"Not too much of a fella. A kindergarten teacher or something. A guy who puts on trade shows."

Sam's father smiled. "I brought weenies for roasting."

"I'll just have a beer," Sam said.

"You'll be happy to have me around," his father said.

By the light of the campfire every thick segment of branch looked like a turd. The book Nadja had thumbed through in Bozeman said that bear scat looked like a human's, so it was hard to tell if a grizzly or a hippie had been in your site before you since they tended to frequent the same places. She stepped on the sticks to make sure they didn't crumble into waste-mud beneath her feet, but she was less worried about the bears that had been there than the ones that would come. She'd started believing that Chris was right, that they'd been stalked by a mama bear. What did she know about bears, other than they were the team that beat the Patriots in the '85 Super Bowl? The meat on the open flame was probably a siren call to every beast in Gallatin County, save the poor bastards kept as roadside attractions in those bear shantytowns thrown up off the state highways.

"How's the weenie?" Sam asked her.

"Perfect with the beer," she answered. The beer was shit too.

The Indian, Rudy, at first told stories of the things he'd hunted when he was a boy out near Billings, in places that were now either twenty-four-hour gas stations with Keno machines or twenty-four-hour Keno casinos with gas pumps. Sam had sat quietly through them, and Chris had written down in the moleskin notebook he kept in his side pocket Rudy's suggestions about where he could still hunt elk, even though Chris couldn't even put the chipmunk he had once accidentally run over on his bicycle to a merciful end, instead pedaling quickly away from its palsied final spasms. Then Chris had taken Rudy's suggestion that he make the forty-five-minute roundtrip to score another case of the Kokanee that had run out at exactly the same time the last Pall Mall was extinguished, and now Chris was sitting beside him like a pet Labrador, swaying in a wind that wasn't blowing from anywhere but Rudy's mouth.

"You folks are from the city, then," Rudy said.

"We're from *a* city," Nadja said. "I wouldn't call it *the* anything."

"Sam's mother is from the city. That's where I found her. A Jewess from . . . where was it again, Sam?"

"Kew Gardens," Sam said after a pause, only when he saw that Nadja was waiting for the answer.

"You know that Indians built New York City? The bridges. The skyscrapers. The things we would never use. You know that?"

"I knew that," Chris said, when it was clear to Nadja that he didn't even know where he was at that moment.

"I went out to build me those skyscrapers. I read about it in *Time*,

Indians building those, whaddyacallem, the World Trade Center. I guess I didn't get to the part in the article that said it was all Mohawks. No Crow there, sir. Heh heh."

"Rudy," Sam said.

"But plenty of Jewesses looking to bring home something for Dad to hate without going all the way black."

"Rudy," Sam said.

"I have to piss," Rudy said. It took him no less than three minutes to stand up from his seat on the ground, turn his back to them, and unzip his pants, and Nadja didn't bother to not stare. His stream roped down into a puddle that crawled toward and then onto his rubber-soled orthopedic sneakers, but he shook neither his sneakers nor his penis off when he was finished. And when he was finished, he turned back around before he had tucked his penis all the way back into his pants, so that Nadja could make out the substantial thing through the smoke and fire before it disappeared again under the blackness of night and Rudy's stonewashed Wranglers.

"Christ, Rudy," Sam said, shaking his head and bowing it between his shoulders at the same time.

"Don't speak of Christ. You're not a man of Christ," Rudy said, and then closed his eyes.

Nadja stared at Chris because she believed it was his duty to get them out of there as he had gotten them into it, but he was also gone from her, too blacked out to even see the trickle of piss snaking its way toward his track pants. She thought about running back to camp and locking herself in the truck, but something was trampling on branches not too far off in the distance, and despite everything she still believed the danger you couldn't see was always worse than the one you could.

"I'm sorry," Sam said. "I'm sorry for him. I'm sorry. I didn't know he would be here."

Nadja shook her head. She looked down at her own shivering body, then back up at Sam. Through the veil of smoke Nadja thought that Sam looked older than he did by daylight. Usually it was the dark that kept things like that hidden, but there was something about campfire. He looked old and he looked sorry. Most men she'd met seemed less sorry the older they grew.

"Are you cold?" Sam asked.

She was still shivering. She wasn't cold.

"Yes," she said.

The inside of the Airstream had enough leaf-shaped air fresheners to make its own forest, but Sam thought it still somehow smelled of work boots. He saw Nadja notice that the bed was made but the little sofa was mussed with an ugly afghan, so she knew where it was that he slept at night. He hoped she understood that all that extra room on the mattress was some kind of failure that he was too tired to challenge by nightfall.

Nadja took a seat on the bench at the table.

"Sorry for the mess," Sam said, though there was no mess. There were no used napkins, no cheap aluminum cookware stacked up by the tiny sink, no photographs of glossy naked strangers or ugly overweight relatives.

"There's no mess," Nadja said.

"What?" he asked.

"There's no mess," she said again, and he smiled. It was easy to lose her voice under the noise of the generator, but he had heard her just fine the first time around. It was just that those were the kindest words Sam had heard from anyone in years.

But he didn't know what came next. He was finding little to say, though he felt it his duty to say something. Something about the forest. The hot spring. He felt like a missionary grown skeptical of his mission, someone hired to proselytize about the wilderness but who had a hard time believing the hype himself. What were two nonbelievers supposed to come up with to talk about, other than all of the non-things?

"I suppose this is not the great camping experience you came all the way out here to enjoy," Sam said, finally.

"I didn't really have any great camping experience in mind," Nadja answered.

Sam tapped on a deck of old, stiff playing cards too brittle to shuffle. He'd bought the pack for the Jokers and hung them on the wall above his toilet.

"Well, what brought you out here if not the great camping experience?" he asked. "Can't imagine you were looking for art museums or French restaurants."

Nadja was sitting on her hands, but Sam felt her feet moving under the table. "Chris wanted to come. He's into this kind of thing. He teaches environmental science at a middle school, so I guess this is like research for him."

"Middle school, not kindergarten," Sam said.

"What?"

"Nothing. Just thinking aloud. What do you do, Nadja?" he asked.

It was the first time he'd said her name since learning it that afternoon, he realized, because it made a new feeling on his tongue. He would try it again soon, but not too soon.

"I take blood," she answered.

"Are you a vampire?"

She didn't laugh. "A phlebotomist."

"Still doesn't explain what brought you out here, unless the blood out here is different somehow."

"Seems like it might be. But like I said, I came with him."

"But why?"

"I don't know, really. That's what boyfriends and girlfriends do. You follow each other around."

"Oh. Of course," Sam said. *Of course*, he said. It didn't seem to him a real answer, but what did he know.

"Chris was pretty taken by him," Sam said, nodding through the wall of the trailer at his father.

"Chris says he's like one-sixteenth Cherokee or something."

"That's what every white person who's not sure they're something else says."

She smiled at that one.

"Rudy Rides the Bear," Sam said.

"What?" she said.

"His name. My father. Rudy Rides the Bear."

"So you're Sam Rides the Bear?"

He shook his head. "My mother changed it back to Hershowitz. Once she realized that the Rides the Bears carried not a proud legacy."

Nothing but generator filled the air for a minute.

"Rides the Bear is nice," Nadja said, when she should've no longer been thinking of it.

"No woman would marry someone with that name," Sam said.

"I would."

Sam's hands stilled on the deck of cards.

"I mean not just for that," she said. "I'm saying it wouldn't matter. Nothing. Never mind."

"What's Chris's family name?" Sam asked.

"Peterson," said Nadja.

"See, that's the kind of name you marry," Sam said.

"Not me. It wouldn't look right with my first name."

"What looks right with your first name?"

"Lots of consonants, probably. The name I already have."

"'Lots of consonants' sounds like the kind of thing girls marry to get rid of."

She shrugged. "The name's not that easy to shake, anyway."

"Ah, a legacy," Sam said.

Nadja pulled the deck of cards from under Sam's hand and spread them out.

"Do you read fortunes?" he asked.

She shook her head.

"Is your father a Rides-the-Bear type?" Sam asked.

"I don't know what type that is," Nadja answered.

"Oh, you know, a drunk. Doing his best to keep the myth of the modern Native person alive."

"My father's not a Native person. He's not even an American."

"Not a drunk?"

"No. A murderer."

Sam looked through the window at his own father, his head balanced on Chris's shoulder to keep him upright as he slept. It was a rare display of affection from Rudy, even if it was inspired simply by gravity.

"I'm sorry," Sam said.

"You didn't do it."

"Who was it?"

"My mother."

Sam nodded, but the only thing he understood was that the evening had not gone as planned, and he wanted it never to end.

"I mean, she was cheating on him," Nadja said. "They both agreed he would kill her if he ever caught her cheating on him."

Sam's pistol was lying atop the television, pointed right at them. He hadn't thought about it when he laid it down before, just as he'd never thought about it any other night since he'd gotten his very first pistol at age fifteen. There was rarely danger attached to it. Nadja's coarse black hair was already matted, thick with what had to be days of grime and at least one leaf, but still, he couldn't picture the tufts dripping with blood. That was him inching toward empathy, he thought: being able to better see the person in the world than imagine the ways in which they could leave it.

"Still, seems kind of unnecessary," Sam finally said. He took Nadja's hand.

She shrugged. "We all have different needs," she said.

"I suppose," Sam answered, but they all felt like one, essentially.

Nadja didn't know what she was doing in there. They'd moved to the couch and Sam held her hand again, and she saw a little mound rise up under his pants. He was forty if a day and this was how he responded to her, like one of Chris's seventh graders would, and so she moved her hand to the mound and held it there, first to cover it up and then because he'd begun chanting, under his breath but discernible, *please please oh please*, and she realized that it was closer to what she was looking for out in Montana than the hot spring, even if it still wasn't exactly right.

Sam's hips began moving slowly, and Nadja's hand stayed where it was, feeling him through the twill. Parts of him were so thin they turned inward. It was almost disgusting, in the way baby animals are right before they're not, and she waited to see if he too would grow into something she wanted to hold onto.

But then he said "Thank you," and meant it, his eyes closed, and immediately she pulled her hand away.

He opened his eyes after a moment but not to look at her. He stared down at himself, looking sorrier than even before.

"You can't say 'thank you,'" Nadja said. "It feels awful."

He nodded but looked about to say it again. How similar gratitude and remorse looked on a face like that.

They were both staring at the door by the time it kicked open and Chris fell into the trailer. He landed on his knees beside Nadja, having tripped on the last stair, and was nearly crying as he tried to kick the door shut.

"The bear," he said, and looked up at Sam.

Sam stood and smoothed his pants down, and it seemed that Chris noticed at first that they wouldn't be smoothed, and he looked back at Nadja. He was still drunk, though, so by the time he made it to his feet he'd forgotten about both the bear and the erection, until he spotted the gun atop the television and pulled it down and held it out toward Sam.

"Kill it," Chris said.

"Hold on now," said Sam. "Hold it. What is it that you think you saw?"

"I did see. All brown, b-big. It's right outside. Sam, you have to kill it!"

"Chris."

"Your father's out there," Chris said.

Nadja's breathing had grown louder than Sam had ever heard her speak.

Sam pulled the gun from Chris's hand, opened the door, and fired blind into the night.

"Dead," Sam said.

Then they heard the scream.

It took several minutes before they realized that the scream was not human. Through the window of the trailer they saw Rudy looking over both shoulders toward the source of the sound, then fold his arms and close his eyes again, convinced that it was coming from a dream he was still somehow having.

"What the hell is it?" Chris asked.

Sam shook his head. He'd aimed for the trees. If that was the sound the trees made he would have to quit real soon.

Nadja was the first one to step out. She crept first toward Rudy and then away so that Sam and Chris knew for sure that he was not the source of the cry, which had quieted by then and was only an occasional groan syncopated with Rudy's heavy breathing.

Sam flashed a Maglite into the woods in the direction he had shot and slowly scanned it until it settled onto a large brown pile whose long legs Nadja saw before she could really make them out.

"What is it?" Sam asked. His arms were shaking, so the light twitched over the animal and made it look like an art film.

"It's the bear, the bear!" said Chris. He fell to his knees and began to vomit, but Nadja knew that it was just the Kokanee that made him do that.

"A moose," Nadja said.

Nadja looked at Sam. She was crying. The sound was too much, the softer it grew.

Again, Sam's look of remorse. "A .22 shouldn't down a moose fifty yards away in one shot," he said.

Nadja shook her head.

"I must've got its leg or something."

"Put it out of its misery," Chris said. "Make that stop. Make it stop."

"Make it stop," Nadja said.

Make it stop, Sam repeated to himself.

It was a clean shot. It echoed through the night.

Feather Ann

The girl's name is Feather Ann, and from the moment you see her you expect her to have scars from diseases people don't get anymore, like measles. You expect her to wear a Band-Aid that flaps around on her shin when the glue finally turns black and quits. You expect her to hang out in the locker room at the YMCA, waiting for the whistle to blow for free swim so she can steal other people's suede moccasins from their cubbyholes. But what you don't expect is for Feather Ann to steal *your* suede moccasins from *your* cubbyhole, and to leave your wallet with the seven dollars and the Ground Round gift card sitting there untouched.

Administration says that if the cockroaches are going to be expelled from the Y then the cockroach high-rises known as the lockers in the girls' room have to go too. Everyone's stuff is now free for the taking, but padlock or not, back when you were a camper the counselors at the Y were too terrifying to dare to cross. You understand things have changed. You are now the counselor, terrifying only to the stray kittens that hide out near your neighbor's muscle car, and further, you can't trust the current campers to operate on the honor system because the only kind of honor system these kids understand is the hand-clap game invented by Honor Jones, a girl with the reading comprehension of a first grader, the breast size of a high school junior, and a legion of devotees among the nine-to-ten-year-old camper group. The nine-to-ten-year-old camper group doesn't recognize or care that while your grad school peers are sitting in quads on liberal arts campuses in coastal Maryland teaching precollegiate summer courses to the brightest 1 percent of children spawned from the wealthiest 1 percent of parents, you came back here, to a city popularly known as the Dirty Water, to teach visual and performing art to them at an underfunded day camp using materials like shipping peanuts and your own single semester of undergraduate theater. It isn't charity but it's nonprofit, which means you could've made more in four weeks behind the counter at Panera Bread than in a whole summer of doing what you're doing. But Panera Bread didn't teach you how to breast-stroke or how to fall in love with a six-foot-six swimming instructor when you were a kid, so you felt like you owed something to the Y. They gave plenty to you despite never having been a young man or a Christian.

The Y is also only a half mile from St. Catherine's, a Catholic hospital with a questionable oncology ward that is caring for your mother, though she was also not a Catholic until very recently.

The point is, you did not expect to leave the summer rich, but you also did not expect to come out of the summer with less than you came in with. That's what you get for expecting anything out of someone like Feather Ann.

At quarter after five you ask Lil at the front desk if Feather Ann was accounted for during free swim.

"It's the counselors' jobs to know where the kids are at during free swim," Lil says.

You ask if Feather Ann has already been picked up by her mother.

"Feather Ann is never picked up by her mother. Feather Ann is picked up by Bus 25 outside of Louie's Pizza," Lil says. "Why are you walking around here barefoot? You looking to catch tetanus?"

You tell her about your moccasins.

"Oh yeah, Feather Ann sure had those. Walking around with

them like flippers on her feet. She told me her mother bought them for her with room to grow."

Feather Ann does not know that your mother bought you those moccasins for your birthday. They were a half size too small for months until finally one day, after the magic mile, they broke in.

By the time you walk the decidedly unmagical half mile to St. Catherine's, your little piggy is rubbed raw from the size-seven water socks Lil lent you for your size-eight feet.

"Those remind me of Action Park. Everybody sloshing around in those little shoes and bikinis two sizes too small for them," your mother says when you enter.

Your mother took you and three friends to Action Park, a New Jersey water park known for its superlative wedgies and personal-injury lawsuits, for your eighth-grade graduation. The two most memorable moments of the day were your friend what's-her-name losing her bandeau top in the wave pool and the stretcher carrying an adolescent boy whose back had been snapped inside a tube whose loop he didn't have quite enough momentum to make it through until the next rider nudged him along at twenty miles per hour. Only that particular ride was closed after that, but your mother made you all leave the park anyway, which made you want to fight with her until you saw that her eyes were watering over not because of chlorine burn.

"He woke up this morning excited for the day. Now he gets to never walk again because he wanted to have a good time with the rest of us idiots," she'd said.

It has now been several weeks since you've seen your mother walk and much longer since she's had a good time with the rest of you idiots. Today she's working on a *TV Guide* crossword and misspelling the names of sitcoms that have been off the air for years in order to get them to fit in the spaces.

"And what did you do today?" she asks, as if to challenge that you've been up to something better.

You tell her about the drawings your seven-to-eight-year-old group made using aluminum foil and cuticle pushers. The website from which you got the idea called it "bas relief," which you read first as "bad relief," and it seemed strange to think of any relief as bad, until last week you watched your mother, floating away on Demerol, seal herself to her pillow with her own saliva.

"What's up with the shoes?" she asks after staring at them for two whole minutes.

Of course you're going to get your moccasins back from Feather Ann, so of course there's no point in telling her you'd been ripped off by a camper to begin with. Uninhibited by the Demerol she could say something racist, even though Feather Ann is a white girl.

You tell her you borrowed the water socks because the bottom of the pool at the Y hasn't been cleaned in a while and that you'd rather not walk in the shallow end without a buffer between you and the tile. You just forgot to change out of them at the end of the day. In the past your mother could always tell when you were lying, but that was dependent on her looking you in the eye.

The kids spray themselves with invisible cans of aerosol disinfectant when Feather Ann comes near. You know that this is true in school, in summer camp, at the playground, anywhere packs of young humans gather to prey on the genetically weaker of their peers. She is clearly poorer than most of the other kids in the group, tubby in the belly not from chronic malnutrition like Sally Struthers's kids but from a lifetime of Head Start breakfasts and free lunches in Sloppy Joe–heavy public school cafeterias. It has not been easy for Feather Ann; you know this, though she does not show it by flinching or looking downward when the kids pull out their invisible aerosol spray cans and back away from her. She is the kind of kid that you'd like to convince of her peers' near-guaranteed future teen pregnancies and the existence of good things outside of city limits, the kind of kid you'd like to encourage to flee as soon as she has the chance, but the girl has stolen your shoes. She must learn first that that is not cool.

Feather Ann does not have a fear of the water but a disinterest so great that the swim instructors fear she will not instinctively doggie-paddle if she wades accidentally into the deep end. In lieu of free swim she rotates between free gym and free nap and free art, but on days when the counselors can't remember or agree upon what her free activity should be, she simply wanders unsupervised around the building until 5:00. Today you find her sitting cross-legged on the floor of the gymnasium, where the residents of the Y are playing basketball in donated T-shirts that bear the name of local baseball teams, each sponsored by a different used-car dealership. She's wearing her usual flip-flops and doesn't look up at you when you sit beside her. When you finally tell her that you'd like to ask her a question, she simply shifts her weight from her left buttock to her right.

You tell her yesterday you had worn your favorite pair of shoes to the Y because they always make your day go a little better, but when you were changing into your street clothes after free swim, you were shocked to find that they were missing.

"Doesn't sound like they made your yesterday go better," she answers.

You ask her, since she did not participate in free swim and various counselors reported seeing her in the locker room during that period, if she knew what might have happened to them.

"I don't have a security cam," she says.

You tell her that the same anonymous sources reported seeing her wearing some worn-in moccasins that appeared a few sizes too large for her feet.

She shrugs. "There's more than one pair of moccasins in the world," she says.

What size are your moccasins? you ask.

"Eight," she says.

Funny, that is exactly my size, you tell her. Your feet appear much smaller than mine.

"Well I'm not giving you mine, if that's what you're asking."

Perhaps she would like to wear them to the Y tomorrow, so that you can compare the similarities between your missing shoes and her new ones.

"Fine," she says.

A stray basketball from the game being played by the Y residents bounces directly into Feather Ann's lap. She doesn't throw it back but waits for the man to retrieve it himself. When he walks away, she tells you that now she'd like to ask you a question.

"Have you ever done it with a black guy?" she asks.

You say, Excuse me?

"I'm only going to do it with black guys," she says. She's staring at the basketball retriever, a wiry man at least forty years, most of which appear to have been very hard. "Their arms are more muscly."

You have nearly been knocked over, though there are no stray balls in your vicinity. You tell Feather Ann that you don't know what "it" she's referring to.

"Then you have bigger problems than your shoes," she says.

You walk away, realizing that it might be true.

The doctors have said that it's exceedingly rare for a woman to die of cervical cancer in this day and age. If this were the fifties, well, that'd be another thing. The doctors also say that cervical cancer is linked to HPV, an STD that's so common that even looking at *Playboy* can transmit it, ha ha, but in all seriousness, they are baffled by how far it advanced before she came in for a pap.

You remember being more shocked to learn your mother had an STD than that she would die from a cancer considered 100 percent curable in its early stages. In middle school there was a poster of a snake entwined around an adolescent girl with the caption *No one can give you VD without your consent.* You had written on it, in what you considered your first moment of activism, What about rape? You left the hospital room that day with the same question, because surely there was no other way your mother had contracted VD. You wondered if having survived such a thing explained anything else about her.

Today she naps through your entire visit. She has always been tired, formerly from the full days put in at Robust Manufacturing and the evenings ringing customers up at Caldor, and Bradlees when Caldor closed, and $2 Or Less when Bradlees closed. She has always been too tired for annual gynecological exams or their precursor, men. Even when you hated her, even when you had to wrap your own arms around your stomach in order to know what it was like to be tucked in and snuggled before bed, you knew it was all for you. When the upstairs neighbor called DCF after hearing you cry for two hours and found you, eight years old at the time, home alone, you tried to explain to the DCF officer that she had only left you because Grandma was too sick to watch you and your mother had to go Christmas shopping, and you obviously couldn't go along. And it was true; the officer wasn't there on Christmas morning, when you unwrapped the rock tumbler you'd wanted since your birthday in April.

You wanted to tell the doctors about the things she'd done right, just like you told the DCF officer. You'd tell them about how she used to bring you to the hardware store that kept two horses in tiny stalls in the back of the garden department so that you could pet their muzzles and feed them the hay that had fallen out of their grasps. Or how she took you fishing at Hop Brook with kernels of canned corn as bait, and although the only thing you ever caught was a saturated maxi pad from the days before ultra-thin with wings, she called you a fisherwoman. Or how she accompanied you to all the liberal arts colleges within driving distance, which in New England meant many many many. How she'd told you, when you said you'd settle for the state university in New Haven, that you shouldn't.

In college you learned how tacky sentimentality is, which was as surprising to you as learning that there are different sizes of infinity. You've forgotten the theorem to prove the latter and don't recall ever having learned anything to prove the former. It was something you just had to take everyone's word on.

Fuck it, you think. Your mother bought you those moccasins, and while they weren't as exciting as that rock tumbler twenty years before, you goddamn well want them back.

Feather Ann stops showing up at the Y. You ask Lil if she's heard anything and she tells you that the Y does not employ truancy officers and that attendance is not mandatory, even though each and every one of the campers is subsidized in some way by the good taxpayers of the State of Connecticut, and you can't help feeling, in a way that you convince yourself is not Republican, that someone should be held accountable. Neither the Christians nor the State of Connecticut provides the Y with enough funding for Lil to stay a minute past her clock-out time, so you wait until she's gone and look up Feather Ann's phone number in her file. The line rings through to a Panda Express on which you hang up twice before the tables are turned and Panda Express star-69s back and hangs up on you. You decide that a home visit might be more productive anyway.

"Miss, did you get your shoes back from Feather Ann yet?" Honor Jones asks you later that day. You were not aware that news had spread among the campers, though you should not have been surprised since they managed to find things to Twitter to each other in computer class that they hadn't found the time to tell each other when they were pliéing in theater arts.

You tell her that she shouldn't accuse people of things that you don't know for sure they did, but what did she hear about it?

"I didn't hear anything, I saw it. Everybody saw her walking around with your shoes."

Why, then, did nobody say anything at the time?

Honor Jones looks at you like you asked her why she didn't report to you that the sky was, in fact, blue. "My mother tells me to mind my own beeswax and don't say nothing about nothing."

It is true that minding one's own beeswax was as basic a tenant as "Look both ways before crossing the street" and "Keep your hands to yourself unless someone starts with you first." It was the kind of code that allowed your neighbor, whose window was separated from your own by approximately twelve feet, to beat his son into a coma, and for the high school guidance counselor to not get put away for soliciting teenaged girls until the week after his full-pension retirement. Still, you thought that Honor Jones would not let Feather Ann get away with theft, if not out of respect for you then out of contempt for Feather Ann.

You tell Honor Jones that you'll be visiting Feather Ann to get to the bottom of it and that she and her friends should also mind their own beeswax about your shoes.

"You're going to Feather Ann's *house*?" Honor Jones asks, horrified, as her flock swarms in to titter along like a Greek chorus. "She lives, like, in a barn."

Nobody here lives in a palace, you say, though half of them do live in Palace Gardens, a prefab complex with a moat of chain link around it.

But Honor Jones is not laughing like her minions. She looks concerned.

"They're just shoes," she says.

Yes, kind of, you say.

The house in which Feather Ann lives does not look as if it deserves an entire dead-end street to itself, yet there are no immediate neighbors. Perhaps the neighbors had sprayed themselves with invisible cans of aerosol and backed away once Feather Ann's family moved in, leaving the house surrounded by vacant lots in which poison ivy and tetanus took the place of modular homes. Like many of the tiny houses in the area, Feather Ann's family looks to have converted the garage into a living space, the outside door to it sealed off with plywood and bathroom caulk instead of a proper wall. That room belongs to Feather Ann, you surmise, when Feather Ann's mother screams out to her in that direction.

You were surprised when both Feather Ann's mother and father answered the door, expecting, like most of your campers, that she was the product of a single-parent home. Peering over their shoulders into the flood of trash over the floor, including several piles of cat turd in various states of decay, you realize that one person alone could not cause as much neglect as went into someone like Feather Ann. They had called out to her before you even had a chance to explain who you were or why you were there, and now you are standing before all of them, looking at none of them, and you think for a moment that maybe Feather Ann should just keep the shoes, both because you would not want them back on your feet after seeing what they had to step through in that house, and because Feather Ann should probably have a little something nice in her life.

But one of the other things Feather Ann should have in her life is a sense of accountability, so you do explain to Mr. and Mrs. Feather Ann about your missing shoes, and that witnesses reported seeing Feather Ann in the missing shoes, and that Feather Ann in fact looks to be wearing them at that very moment, the toes of them stuffed the way other girls stuffed their bras.

"Did you take those shoes from this lady, Feather Ann?" Feather Ann's mother asks.

"No," she answers.

"So who are your witnesses? Some little girls who don't like my daughter?" Feather Ann's mother asks, despite very clearly seeing what was on Feather Ann's feet and almost certainly knowing that she had not bought them for her daughter. The father is also staring at the shoes from the table, where he ashes a GNC cigarette into the lid of a giant Atomic Fireball container which sits like a centerpiece on a table that is—inexplicably, given the crap on the floor—otherwise empty. Every time he looks about to say something, he lifts the cigarette back to his mouth and puffs out carbon monoxide instead of words.

It is sad and a little surprising to learn that Feather Ann's mother understands that Feather Ann is not popular with her peers, though the chance of things turning out differently was slim, considering the environment and the thirdhand puff-painted sweatshirts in which she was raised. But you are not here to judge, only to retrieve your shoes, you remind yourself, and anyway, it could be that Feather Ann's parents are simply very messy people.

But then Feather Ann's mother begins speaking, and you understand that her problems are not as simple as being a collector of trash.

"You people will do anything to get in this house. I don't know what the hell else you want from us. We got rid of the dog. You already took the baby. Feather Ann helps us, okay? We need her. We do right by her."

You tell her that you don't doubt that, even though silently you do.

"I bet all your little nanobot friends are sneaking into the house right now. You think I need to see them to know they're there? I can feel them. They make my teeth hurt."

The father has walked away and you would like to do the same thing in the other direction, because you don't know what a nanobot is but you know that the mention of them makes you suddenly and deeply sad. She sounds much like the people who sleep on benches on the green downtown, people who clearly spend hours on the Internet at the public library, researching conspiracies for half the day and posting incoherent responses to unrelated news articles for the other half of the day. They retire to their benches in the late afternoon as you're leaving the Y and spit on the ground after you walk by, rinsing away whatever malicious dust your feet have left behind. Feather Ann's mother wants to spit on you now, you can see, and you almost respect the restraint she shows by keeping it in. You tell her again that you're simply a counselor at the Y, this time not to justify your showing up at the house but to reassure her that you bear no nanobots.

"The Y? Great, church and state all in one. Just what we need."

You are neither church nor state, you say, just a visual and performing arts teacher for eight weeks in the summer, and you are not looking to take away anybody's dog or baby or Feather Ann, just the shoes that Feather Ann is wearing that don't belong to her.

"Like you need them," Feather Ann's mother says. "Like you don't get everything you want."

It is the worst thing she could have said, and you would have preferred being spit on to hearing it because it is not the first time you've heard it, and you've never once understood it. Your friends back in middle school, after they'd returned from the trip to Action Park, repeated for weeks how lucky you were to have a mother who'd drive you all the way to New Jersey just because you wanted to show off your new boobs in a swimsuit. After high school, the new friends that you'd managed to make after your middle school friends spread slutty rumors about you told you you'd never understand what it's like to work third-shift with a newborn because you'd gotten to go to college and play around with rich twats instead. The rich twats in college worried that they'd never be able to live up to their parents' expectations of them and said you didn't know how lucky you were that you'd already gone farther than anybody ever thought you would. You wonder what is wrong with you, why you have never appreciated being such a lucky girl, and why all you want to do is mope around and worry about your eighteen-dollar shoes.

Feather Ann has returned to the room, this time in her flip-flops, and she empties the Atomic Fireball ashtray and returns it to the table. You think you understand why Feather Ann dreams of walking in soft brown suede into the arms of a strong black man, but you don't give her permission to change back into your shoes, nor do you demand their return for a final time. You know that you will simply replace your suede moccasins with an identical pair from the discount department store where the last pair came from, and tomorrow will still feel exactly as yesterday had felt, the ground still crumbly under your feet.

You tell Feather Ann's mother that you're sorry to have bothered her, and she closes the door on you, but behind her you see Feather Ann's shock, as if she'd been waiting for that apology all her life.

In old movies the staff at Catholic hospitals were all nuns, but in real life they are just the weary, overworked associate's degree holders who staff every other bureaucratic agency in the world. They ask if your mother had made arrangements, and because you want to see them try not to lose their tempers in the face of your grief, you want to answer, What kind of arrangements? Flower arrangements? No, she did not make flower arrangements. She did not bring baskets of fruit cut to resemble tulips along to baby showers. At baby showers she wore fancy tracksuits and made white wine sangria that she insisted was fine to drink in the third trimester. She brought home the little mesh bags of Jordan almonds offered at every single baby shower ever hosted and saved them for years on her dresser, as if they were eggs that were waiting to hatch. They were duds; they never did anything except lure tiny winged insects that never managed to bore through the taffeta.

Instead you tell the bureaucrat that yes, your mother did make arrangements, giving her credit for the work with the funeral home your uncle did a week ago, before your mother was fully convinced that this was really going to happen.

Because you too had not been convinced that this was really going to happen, you did not clear out the four-year-old jars of dill relish and pickled beets in the refrigerator to make way for the trays of baked ziti that are donated to you following the funeral reception at the VFW hall. In three days you only manage to eat the burnt cheese crust off of a two-inch square, and after you vomit that up, you decide that it might be best for you to get out of the house for a while. Being out of the house for a while then convinces you to get out of the house for good, so you check yourself into the Super 8 on Scott Road only to find that your nausea returns whenever you sit still for more than thirty seconds, and is nearly critical after the thirty-six hours straight you lay on top of the flowered Super 8 coverlet, neither eye turned to the Weather Channel, which remains on for the duration.

You decide to return to the Y for the final four days of the camp session.

The first thing you think when you see Lil is that you never returned her water socks, and you know that this is also the first thing she is thinking, though she only says good morning and touches your hand for a moment before turning back to her giant IBM terminal that was clearly donated by a neighboring law firm fifteen years ago. The machine looks like a prop, what filmmakers in the 1980s thought the 2000s would look like, large with sharp corners and heavy on the matte beige. Instead, the 2000s saw computers and denim shorts get very small, and very little else changed, especially here in the Y, where campers still wear their hair in braids and take field trips to Hammonasset State Park, even on days where the water is off-limits due to jellyfish infestations. The senior citizens in the hot tubs today look much like those who soaked their weary bones fifteen years ago, though those seniors must be long dead, their skirted swimsuits now draped on Salvation Army hangers, the Lycra as slack as the Irish Catholic skin that once filled them.

Fifteen years ago your mother was your age, and managed to care for a child and a dozen philodendron. Now you have managed to lose two of the campers under your watch in arts and crafts and do not know what to say to the counselor who asks why the sixteen who responded at your roll call has been reduced to fourteen in his swim class.

It is not until you are told that you should step outside for some fresh air that you see Feather Ann, who has apparently stopped attending summer camp for good and instead loiters across the street in the green, near the rearing brass horse oxidized to a green you associate with sunken treasure chests, though the city has not been underwater but for the Great Flood of 1955. She lies splayed against the base of the statue, her T-shirt knotted below the breastbone, sunburning her name onto her belly using a stencil you remember her creating from construction paper in your visual arts class while the rest of the campers worked on macaroni art. Her eyes appear to be closed, but when you attempt to skirt her, she says, "Are you looking for me?"

No, you tell her.

"Oh," she says, and lifts the stencil to check her progress. The skin beneath is as white as chalk against the pink boil of the surrounding flesh.

Where did you get your name? you ask.

"I don't know, my mom made it up. Where did you get yours?" she asks.

You don't bother to clarify that you meant the stencil.

Same here, you say, and shield your eyes against the sun.

Two Assholes

When Maureen took those Microsoft Office classes down at Dr. Professor a few months back, she started a spreadsheet of the reasons she had to divorce my ass. She gave weights to the reasons, rated them on a scale from one to ten, used some kind of built-in voodoo math function, and handed it in for an assignment. Handed the goddamned thing in to the class so that all the other middle-aged ladies could bear witness to the sinking ship she sailed on, except why in the world would these women care when they're all in there training to be secretaries for the same reason she is? That's the way she was, though, thinking the whole world was just on the edge of their seats waiting for her to say something, when the closest she ever actually came to that kind of rapture was when she showed off her titties at the 1986 Terryville swap meet after one Meister Bräu too many, and even then nobody cared what was coming out of her mouth.

Those titties look almost as good now as they did back when she was twenty-two, I'll give her that.

So that spreadsheet, she left it out on the refrigerator when she got an A-minus on it. "It's scientifically proven," she said and pointed to it. "We need a divorce."

I looked down the columns. Even a junior math dropout like me knew that thing was flawed. How can you come up with a mean of somebody's worth when all you got listed is their negative characteristics? What about that Cutless Supreme she was driving? What about that front and back lawn, mowed to perfection every Saturday afternoon? What about having a lawn to mow in the first place instead of the blacktop playground of a housing complex, like what Tony had to play on until he was two? That's not good enough for our kid, I told her, and I put in the overtime to live up to my word. I still remember that screw she gave me the first night in our new place. It was art, man, a genuine soul-stirring movement. And she cried. Wept for joy at not sharing any walls with a Puerto Rican family of twelve, not sharing the playground with any teen-aged punks chaining their pit bulls to the monkey bars when Tony was playing four feet away in the sandbox. And she loved me hard. Hard—her word, not mine. "I love you hard, Viktoras Matascavas," she said, and she went down on me for a full ten minutes without even a groan of complaint, and then mounted on top of me so sure and steady I could barely move under her weight. That's the moment that's gonna flash in front of me when I die, coming so hard my heart hurt, falling asleep with my dick still inside her. I bet that's when Tonia came to be, man. That shit was too pure, too good for nothing to come of it.

And now, reason number one: *Vic leaves cups of spit from his disgusting chew in the living room where I am supposed to relax but where I can't because I have to clean it up when it spills over, which it always does. 6.3 points. Tony joined ROTC to put himself through school because Vic told him community college until his third year, because Vic evidently doesn't think his kids are smart enough for a real education just because he wasn't. 9.7 points. Tonia, who is six-foot-one and who could be a model but not with those teeth. 8.9 points. Thinking nobody else might need to use the bathroom on Sundays for two hours at a time. 6.5 points.*

The rest of that list—I mean, if she would just calm herself down she'd see my point in it all. Tony was a good kid, but I guarantee you he'd have been calling me up asking me to get him a job at Ferlingheti Bros. after two semesters if he hadn't dropped out and gone active Army instead. And I love my Tonia, don't get me wrong, but any reasonable person knows them damn braces aren't covered or cheap. A little snaggle gives them character anyway, right? But that thing about the bathroom, come on. That had nothing to do with any decision I made. It was completely irrational to put it on that list, just downright mean. She used to think it was funny when I'd head on up there with the Sunday Register and make it through sections A through F plus some circulars before I even got a pellet out. Called it "going to church" and signed the cross over herself when I passed her in the hallway.

This, I thought, *this I can fix, Maureen*. Yeah, it was only 6.5 points, but you gotta understand where I was at. Listening to that talk for months now, out of nowhere it seemed, Maureen all turned around on me as if maybe the old Italian lady whose mailbox I accidentally ran over with my pump truck put the *malocchio* on me or something.

So I made an appointment with Dr. Raad, a guy whose name I knew only because I made out plenty of co-pay checks to him when the kids were growing up. Never saw his face myself until that day in the office, and believe me, with the kinds of tests he was running he wasn't somebody I was wanting to look in the eye anyway. That's love, I felt like Maureen should know: three days of fasting and two hours of prodding in places I never even let her get at.

"So, Mr. Matascavas," Dr. Raad said after all the poking, like that was a time for small talk, "you've had trouble using the bathroom your whole life?"

"Yeah, more or less," I said. It would've been nice to have had to go more often, like some of the guys at work who go off to the Port-a-Let for twenty minutes at a time on the clock while I'm being punished with no breaks because I don't shit or smoke. One more thing hard work will get you: forty extra minutes of hard work a day and not an extra cent to show for it.

"Okay," he said. I finally looked at him straight on, and his face screwed up so tight his eyebrows practically crossed over each other in the middle of his face. And I'm thinking, What's he so worked up about? What's out there to shock a doctor? And then I'm thinking:

cancer. Gotta be cancer. I never been one for doctor visits, never been one to get sick, but suddenly it dawns on me—God's just been saving up for something big. A lifetime of constipation and no harm's gonna come of it? All that unloaded crap isn't stewing in there, hardening up into some kind of toxic cookie? And then I'm thinking, no way Maureen or any human being with half a heart could leave a man with cancer. She'll be combing her fingers through my hair when I puke chemotherapy out into the toilet bowl. I was practically smiling by the time he finally came out with it.

"Mr. Matascavas, I am a bit concerned. It's too soon to jump to conclusions, of course, but we did detect some kind of mass during the colonoscopy. Not polyps, which is what we usually see, but—"

"But what?" I said.

"Well, we're not quite sure yet. Most growths that we find are benign, mind you, and even the ones that aren't can often be completely removed with a simple surgery."

"Uh-huh," I said.

He stopped for a second, then said, "Your growth does appear to be quite large, however."

"Which means?" I said.

He shrugged. "It doesn't *necessarily* mean anything. Just that we need to run more tests."

What "It doesn't *necessarily* mean anything" actually means is that some shit is certainly going down, that if you're one out of the million to get away with this thing scot-free then you best start going back to church and kissing that sweet Jesus's feet for the blessing you've received. Only I grew up Catholic, so I'd place my money on certain suffering over scot-free any day.

"Let's schedule some follow-ups," Dr. Raad said.

"Sure thing, Doc," I said.

It was a beautiful suffering, for a little bit anyways.

"Maureen," I told her when I got home, "I got something to tell you."

She kept working on opening up a can of lima beans to dump into whatever's-in-the-cabinet soup.

"So tell it," she said.

"The doctor says, well, I got some kind of growth up there in my colon or wherever. Doctor thinks it's cancer."

"What?" She lost her grip on the lima beans and the lid sliced right into her finger. "What do you mean, cancer?" Cut and everything, she took the meanness out of her voice, brought back the confectionary sugar tone she used with the kids when they were down with the chicken pox. I wanted to kiss her, but I figured I shouldn't press my luck.

"I don't know," I said. "Cancer cancer. Need more tests." I didn't mention worst or best case to her, worst being something you don't talk about and best being something that sounded pretty much perfect: surgery, a few weeks off from work, a few weeks together with Maureen watching television, eating those cinnamon rolls from the tube while we kick back and catch up on *Survivor*, and I wouldn't even fall asleep five minutes into it because I won't have gotten up at four thirty that morning. Maybe a few extra days to take her back to Lake George, so she could remember that time way back when she was good to me, maybe even a second honeymoon on one of those fancy cruises she always wanted to take down in St. Wherever, Virgin Islands. Maybe I'd sign up for one of those continuing ed classes at Naugatuck Valley Community Technical College that Maureen was always talking about, or at least not give her a hard time about spending my money on one for herself. I even thought about calling up Tonia and telling her that Dad will help her with the payments on some braces if she still wants them, even if I figured that at eighteen she wouldn't.

Maureen paced a couple of times around the island in the kitchen, not looking at me, saying, "What? What?" and spilling blood onto the floor. "Shit," she said, and look—instead of using a napkin, instead of a paper towel, she pulled the spreadsheet from the fridge and wrapped her finger up in it, a beautiful freaking tourniquet to stop that rush of blood. And then she hugged me. I can't remember the last time I got one of those. When she finally pulled back from it, there were tears in her eyes. Those I were used to, but not this kind. Not the kind I liked to see.

"It'll be alright, baby," I told her, and when she buried her head into my chest, I'm telling you, man, I meant what I said.

The whole time they were running the tests, me and Maureen were getting along just fine. She took the spreadsheet off the refrigerator, made some real dinners, actually came to bed with me and let me spoon her for a while.

"How does kielbasa sound tonight?"

"You comfortable? You want a pillow?"

"Tony called today. Sends his love."

It was like a symphony, hearing her say things like that. Nice things. Not things like, "If only I'd finished up nursing school . . ." or "Tony and Tonia—those are your kids, remember?" or just the dead silence that could go on for days. And I wasn't worried. Feeling better than ever, actually. Still not shitting much, but I figured the next surgery would take care of that. Even if it wasn't cancer, it was a close enough call to scare Maureen back to me, her provider, her husband. When we walked back into the doctor's office for the results of the biopsy they did, we were holding hands. A couple. An honest-to-goodness married couple.

The fancy doctor at Yale–New Haven was tall, blond, probably a Vanderbilt or something from the looks of him. Only, when he walked in he looked a lot like Raad, what with his eyebrows all cinched together like they were.

"Well, Mr. Matascavas," he said, "you are cancer free."

Maureen exhaled so quiet that I only heard it because I was listening for it. Her hand loosened its grip on me a little, so I took up the slack and held onto hers tighter.

"What you have is indeed a tumor, a benign one. But it's also an unusual one."

Maureen stared straight ahead at him, me at her, and the doctor into his chart.

"We call your type of tumor a teratoma. Teratomas are tumors that contain a variety of cell tissues, unlike most tumors that only contain tissue specific to the region where the tumor grows. There are different kinds of teratomas within this category, but what you have is a mature teratoma, which thankfully is seldom malignant."

"English, doctor?" Maureen said, still staring straight at him as if I couldn't ask for myself.

"Teratomas are—" The doctor stopped, trying to think of the smallest words in his vocabulary so that people like me and Maureen could understand him. "Teratomas develop from an unfertilized egg. For whatever reason, even though there has been no fertilization, cell division takes place and the tumor grows tissue that you would normally see in a developing fetus. It can contain things like bones, teeth, hair, brain tissue, eyes, even organs. You see here," and he pointed, "that's why your X-ray here appears to show you have two, um, rectums. Mind you, everything is randomly arranged and doesn't look like a fetus and will never ultimately grow into an independently functioning human being, but it can continue to, I don't want to say mature—let's just say they can continue to develop and grow."

I admit, I got caught up on the two rectums. Here's my little Junior, I'm thinking, all grown up with an asshole of his very own. And I knew straight away what Maureen was thinking when she slipped her hand completely out of mine: here I thought I got stuck with one asshole, and now it turns out I've got to deal with two. Even under her blush, always a little on the heavy side, her color drained until the veins underneath poked right through.

"Mr. Matascavas, by 'mature' teratoma we don't mean that it's mature in any kind of developmental way. But by the size of the tumor, we do think it's been growing for quite some time. An entire lifetime, perhaps. Because sacrococcygeal teratomas like yours are normally discovered at birth, even neonatally with today's technology. It's very rare, although not completely unheard of, for adults to make it to adulthood without them being discovered. In your case, it's apparently positioned in a way that it hasn't completely impaired any of your vital functions, so without regular checkups I guess it just wouldn't have been suspected."

Maureen wasn't even looking at the doctor anymore. She'd turned to the diagram on the wall of the man cut in half, his hands spread out on the sides of him like he was dancing some kind of jazz number. I wanted to punch the guy in the drawing just like I would have if he was some guy she was checking out in the bar. Maureen, always with that wandering eye. Always thinking she could do better, her with her continuing ed and nice titties and me with my gut and a creature in my belly. The guy in the drawing didn't have no monsters growing inside him. He didn't have a gut from eating Arby's too many days a week. He didn't have any responsibilities, no job, nothing to make him tired and cranky even though a sensible person would appreciate that the crankiness is a sacrifice for his family, not an attack against it. I don't have to be happy to wake up at three a.m. to make a pour at four thirty, but they damn well should be happy about it. That's the mortgage, Maureen. That's the good life I promised you.

But then the doctor cinched it. "I'll be honest with you, Mr. Matascavas, this is something we don't see often, and usually in women. You are highly unusual."

And I saw Maureen right then adding to her spreadsheet. *Vic is highly unusual. 10 pts.* If he'd have said special, maybe it wouldn't have been so many points against me. If he'd have said sick, maybe that spreadsheet would've been deleted right off the computer. But unusual, that was Maureen's one-way ticket outta there. All my life with her I been trying to do what a man should, take care of his family and stand proud in front of his mowed lawn and what do I get? A case of monster-belly, a little Junior growing in me right where Tony grew inside of Maureen. Maureen's mother was always saying the kids took after Maureen, and under her breath she'd be saying *Thank God for that*. Now I got a kid of my very own and he turns out to be nothing but a bundle of fur and hair and rectums, some kind of brainless, mute beast sucking down the stray kielbasa that my belly missed. All my life I been working hard, thinking I'm doing right, and this is my legacy? For nothing, all for nothing. I saw it when Maureen finally turned back at me and stared like she was nearsighted, like maybe she recognized me but wasn't sure enough to risk waving. So I did it first. I waved at her with a little grin, like we were neighbors running into each other in the deli line, and just like I suspected she looked away, back at the jazz dancer with his streamlined physique, showing off his perfect, healthy little organs arranged just like they should be.

"I'm sure this is something we can take care of surgically," the doctor said.

"You just take care of cashing your bloated paycheck," I said. "I'll take care of myself." Because right then I knew that's what I'd be doing. Me, myself, and my little undeveloped egg, my demented, deformed little Junior, heating up our Dinty Moore in the microwave and trying to keep awake for late-night Skinemax while Maureen graduates from Dr. Professor and takes a job as an administrative assistant, then moves on to personal assistant, *real* personal assistant, telling some schmuck who drives a Suburban just to tow around his personalized golf clubs that she loves him hard, a guy who tucks in his shirt even on weekends, who runs for some local municipal position and loses to a lesbian because his smear campaign backfired and he doesn't even care because he never really cared to begin with, and why should he because his high-definition plasma TV is a high-definition plasma TV whether he's town comptroller or not. A life of shower gel instead of lava soap. A life where Tony drops out of UConn instead of Naugatuck Valley Community Technical College, a life where Tonia took a boyfriend to prom instead of a boy who came out of the closet at age eleven. A *better* better life than the one I gave her. And who cares if that life I gave her left me with almost nothing, just a shriveled, half-a-man holding out for whatever leftovers come his way.

I heard Maureen calling after me when I opened the door and walked right out. "Vic. Vic. Viktoras Matascavas, come back here now!"

I'll come back if you do, I thought to myself, but neither one of us made the move. I just kept on walking straight out to the car and waited for her to hitch a ride back with me.

A few minutes later she did. "Why the hell did you walk out like that?" she said.

I didn't say anything back.

"What the hell is wrong with you? I mean besides having a creature living in your belly, what the hell is wrong with you?"

Nothing again.

"You've got to get rid of that thing. You can't just leave it there."

"Why not?" I finally said.

"Because it's *disgusting*."

"It's not cancer. It's not going to kill me."

"It will kill me. I will *die* if I have to sleep next to you knowing that thing is living inside you."

"You don't have to sleep next to me. You can sleep anywhere you want. You can sleep with some douchebag who talks about his clientele and his client base. You can call him Gary. Because that's going to be his name. His name will be Gary."

Maureen looked at me like the thing inside my belly crawled out and was sitting there on my right shoulder.

"What are you talking about? Is this thing getting to your brain or what?"

"Yeah, probably," I said. "Why don't you add that to your spreadsheet?"

She didn't say anything back right away.

"I'm sorry about the spreadsheet," she finally said. "That was mean."

"Yeah," I said. "Sorry." I should've snapped up an apology,

because those were rarer than Halley's Comet from Maureen, but I didn't feel like it. Because like Halley's Comet, it was damned disappointing. Waiting and waiting for something nice from her, and in the end it was just a few seconds of cloud-covered fizzle. A weak little *sorry*. What about a big strong *thank you for taking care of us, for letting me stay home and raise the kids so they could grow to not be little punks, for buying me that computer, which I then turned around and used against you with my fancy A-minus spreadsheet*. Nope, just cloud-covered fizzle that amounted to nothing. So I felt like being mean back, ganging up on her, me and little Junior in my belly versus Maureen.

"Sorry," I said again, in case she didn't hear me, in case she missed the ironicality in my voice. But if she didn't hear the first one then she really didn't hear the second, because she was so far away by then she might as well have been in a different car. She might as well have been in Acapulco, sipping on a coconut rum and suntanning the stretch marks on her belly clear away, Gary checking the stocks in a beach chair right beside her.

But that Maureen—you knew she wasn't gonna stay quiet for long. Yeah, she might've kept her mouth shut the whole forty minutes back, but that's because she was devising a new kind of plan in her head, some way to sabotage this and make Junior out to be something I hatched just to torture her. I was expecting her to call her mother when we got back and tell her all about what I'd done to her, how I'd been born with a monster egg inside of me, and how it's been growing the whole time we were married, and *how could he do this* and *what if this was passed down to the kids* and *he's named it, Ma, he's gone ahead and named it Junior.*

But oh no. Maureen is smarter than she lets on, I'll give her that. She knew her mother didn't hold any sway over me. So when the phone rang and Maureen answered and said, "Oh, hey, Whitey," man, if I was thinking on my feet I would've snatched the phone out of her hands so quick it would've let a burn mark on her palm.

But like usual, I was thinking on my ass, lying there on the couch and dozing off to one of those court TV shows.

"Oh yeah, he's fine," I heard her say. "Well, except for the tumor isn't really a tumor, it's an unfertilized egg that's grown into some kind of creature with teeth and hair and an asshole, and Vic has decided it's fine where it is and doesn't want it removed, and he's calling it Junior like it's a fucking pet, and he thinks this is all just so funny."

I ran over to the phone and hit disconnect before she had a chance to get anything else out.

"Your check is ready," she said to me.

"I know about the check," I said. I'm not one of those guys that pushes women around, but if ever there was a moment I come close to it, that was it. That mouth of hers, somebody's got to shut it, and force seemed like a pretty reasonable way. "What the fuck did you just do?" I yelled, the kind of yell I usually reserved for the kids, which means I hadn't even used it in a couple years. It's a good yell, a nice full baritone one, I have to say. It felt good to get it out again.

"What? What, are you ashamed? Can't tell people about Junior? You know why? Because it's disgusting and you need to get rid of it. You need to come to your fucking senses," she yelled back, hers more soprano but just as impressive.

On cue there's a rumble from my belly. "What's that, Junior?" I said. "You think Maureen is being an ungrateful witch? That she doesn't appreciate everything I done for her and the kids and is going to use a tumor as an excuse for why she can't love me anymore?"

Then she looked as if I had hit her, as if she knew how close I'd come to it and just the thought of it set a big welt on her face.

"Viktoras, Junior's been in this picture, what? Four hours? And you want to say this is why I don't love you? After spelling it out for you on the goddamned refrigerator for months?"

"Oh, so not shitting is a reason to divorce a man? You want to flush twenty-two years and two kids down the crapper because I don't got much else to flush?"

"How petty do you think I am? Don't you see the point in all that?"

"No, Maureen, for honest I don't see the point."

She clammed up for a minute, and the red that spreads over her cheeks when she's mad faded into pink, something almost pretty.

"You never ask me anything, Vic, you haven't let me talk to you in twenty years. I wanted to fight. I wanted you to see that list and stick up for yourself and tell me I'm wrong so I could prove I was right or something, goddamned *anything*. Then I wanted to make up and for you to ask me how I learned how to do that stuff on the computer, which three months ago I couldn't turn on."

Her tone right then—it was quiet, musical almost. I heard Maureen sing before. It was real pretty, real airy and floaty. She played Maria in her high school's production of *West Side Story* a couple months before I met her, and I could still see Maria in her. She felt pretty back then, oh so pretty. I wonder what she felt now. I had no fucking clue, myself. She looked pretty, that I could tell you. Or her, I could've told her. But I didn't. It wasn't the right time, you know? This was a fight. This was a time to say mean things, right? A time to get out what you have to suck in when your boss reams you, or when your coworkers bust your balls a little too hard, or when the guy in the BMW cuts you off on I-84 and you know his 5-series wouldn't be any match for your pump truck but you can't run him down because you're the one who'd lose your job and get sued for a million when all the douchebag had to do was wave, just one tiny little wave to acknowledge he was sorry or grateful or something.

"Aw, right," I said. "Just go to hell."

Go to hell. Not a great line, right? An oldie, a classic, not all that powerful, I thought. But it seemed to hit Maureen pretty hard, harder than the open hand I almost threw at her would've. She looked up at me like I was the devil himself, like she'd already gone to hell and what a stupid thing to say that was. Then she walked away. Walked away from a fight. She said she wanted to talk, right? But she just walked away.

Maureen didn't go to hell. Of course not. She went to her mother's and I stayed here. We stayed here—me and Junior, I mean, still waiting for that front door to open, waiting for some door somewhere to open. Tell that story to your buddies at work, the one about the guy with two assholes, I bet you'll get yourself a good laugh. Just do it when you think we're not listening through the open window of our pump truck, or when we're concentrating so hard on lubing up that diesel engine that we could never possibly hear you chuckle. Nah, we can't hear a word you say. We never at all heard a thing.

Two-Step Snake

The hell with just knowing. Hilary's mother always told her she would *just know it* when she met the right guy, but Hilary also knew that the guy her own mother had *just known* about didn't stick around to see his own kids eat nothing but SpaghettiOs Meatballs or hear them say their first curse words by their third birthdays. Hilary didn't have any hunches about Jack. She knew exactly what she loved about him and let the sum total dictate that she should marry him. It was a goddamned algorithm, it was so precise. The name Jack, for example—it was an excellent name. A movie-character name. She could say, "This is my husband, Jack" and mean it when she squeezed his arm because it was just that sexy. Or the ridge where his hip met his torso like he was a marble statue pumped suddenly warm with blood—it was a line, it was *really* there. She sketched him sometimes as he watched TV on the futon, thinking maybe she would have made it all the way through that life-drawing class if only the teacher had kept Jack as the nude model through the entire session instead of switching to the beasty co-op produce manager whose real name Hilary'd bet a thousand dollars wasn't Zinnia. Jack alternated Value Meals # 3 and 5, the only sit-up he'd ever done was reaching for the remote, and still he looked like that. A body like Jack's was proof of God—and that God didn't give a shit about justice.

And there were the snakes: Hemachatus haemachatus, Naja siamensis, Causus rhombeatus, and the lovely, deadly Bothrops atrox—all venomous enough to kill them a few times over, all living in glass aquariums in their bedroom closet. Hilary never complained even though her clothes hung from a brass pipe in the basement and smelled of must and mice turd straight out of the dryer. She loved Jack because he loved those snakes. She loved the look on her mother's face when she told her she'd run off and married a guy who bred venomous reptiles. She loved watching Jack incubate hatchlings in a twenty-five-gallon paint bucket he called the Ranch, handling them with a tenderness he showed only with them and sometimes, every once in a while, herself. She even loved the explanation he gave her when they first met, when she asked why snakes. "They're just these little tubes with no arms and no legs and tiny little brains," he'd said, "and people are scared to death of them. That's pretty g.d. cool."

Yeah, it was pretty g.d. cool, she'd thought. Only now the sum of what she loved about him didn't add up to much, didn't even clear the red, and the name and the hip and even the snakes didn't mean anything better than just knowing. Instead of breeding snakes he was trying to breed Jacks, when, if he'd been paying attention, he would've known all along that knocking Hilary up was not okay. Now Hilary stared into the tank of the *Bothrops atrox*, the fer-de-lance that Jack had raised from a tiny worm into the five-foot pit viper that she was today, and Hilary wished that she had the snake's venom, wished she could lash out and take down half a dozen Jacks in one gnash of her teeth.

Hilary dug under the sink looking to make a withdrawal from the lobster pot where she kept the balled-up dollar bills the rich Wesleyan frat boys left her for every beer she cracked open for them down at the Cape Codder. Problem was the money she wasn't there. She darted back into the bathroom, where she'd just retched into the commode for ten straight minutes, and there was nothing in the magazine rack they called the Safety Deposit Box either. The money kept running off, looked like. That's what must've happened to it, it up and grew legs and ran off like their dog had when Hilary went to Lowell, Massachusetts, for her grandfather's funeral. She came back three days later and Squiggy was gone, and in Squiggy's place on the couch was Jack, all curled up like the corgi that should've been lying there.

"Where's Squiggy?" she'd asked him.

"Man, I don't know. I come home a couple days ago and he wasn't there. I think the screen door's busted."

"The screen door's been busted since we moved in!" Hilary shrieked, and she cried up and down the streets calling out Squiggy's name for two hours a day for three days until finally some neighbor sent over a patrol unit who told her to either put up some flyers or else he'd write out a ticket for a noise ordinance he knew she couldn't pay.

Especially not when the money kept running off. She could count on forty dollars running off at least once a week, or more like forty dollars going up in smoke by way of the acrylic pipe named *Sweetpuff*, according to the Gaelic lettering etched across its surface. But mostly they were just fine. They rented a little house with a little yard in Town Plot, where their little Squiggy could bury his little bones and everything could be fine in the little, tiny way she'd ever dare hope for. She couldn't remember ever asking Jack for anything besides to shut it when his snoring got too loud.

"Son of a bitch," she yelled and kicked open the screen door so hard that it went from busted to busted clear off, not that it ever really kept corgis in or mosquitoes out anyway. Hilary paced the fence around the backyard like a prisoner on rec break. She'd already made the appointment, and when they'd told her two weeks she'd cried, pleaded with them wasn't there anything sooner? They'd told her, No sweetie there wasn't, and Calm down sweetie you'll be fine, and she couldn't convince them that she wouldn't be. Not with a nausea so huge it spilled out of her stomach and coursed through her blood to every reach of her body until it seeped from her pores in a sweat as thick and cold as the Jell-O she made the mistake of trying to eat that morning. Not when she made a living, if you could call what she did living at that point, standing on her feet for ten hours on a floor lined with spilled PBR and underaged puke instead of linoleum. Not when her husband had spent the last two hours asleep instead of holding her hair back while she leaned over the toilet, who never even bothered to notice that she'd been sick for two weeks straight, who instead had spent the first six hours of his waking day keeping watch over two mating fer-de-lances and spent the last six twiddling the same four chords on a wretchedly out of tune Yamaha steel-string instead of stroking her leg when she sat down next to him and draped it over his lap.

And not when she noticed the blue tarp jutting out beside the tool shed. She hadn't really noticed how much it didn't belong until that moment. She moved across the yard, the morning frost still crunching underneath her feet an hour into the afternoon, and lifted a corner. An aquarium, a giant aquarium with plenty of room for an alligator or two if he wanted them, which he probably did. Probably took that leftover money he stole from her to put toward a down payment on an anaconda that he'd feed live dogs to. That's probably what happened to Squiggy, she figured. Bastard ran out of rabbit carcasses and couldn't be bothered to get his lazy ass to the carcass vendor to get more. Probably chopped him right up and nuked him in the microwave and fed him to all the hungry fer-de-lances who didn't care whether they were eating rabbit or dog or human baby, so long as it was warm.

Hilary went inside and sat beneath the afghan on the futon. The fire in the pit of her belly set a fresh batch of nausea to simmer, and she began to sweat so fierce that her shirt got drenched and set her off shivering like a teacup in her grandma's hand. But she wasn't going to puke. She was going to keep it down until he came home so he could see what he'd done to her, maybe let it out when the door opened half an hour later and Jack stepped inside dressed in a T-shirt and sandals as if August had stuck around just for him. But when he did walk in, her stomach steadied instead, her insides solidifying into granite, something impenetrable that he would never break through, not ever again.

"Hey, babe," he said when he saw her.

"Whose aquarium is that outside?" she asked as calm as anybody who asked a question without any right answer should be.

"What? Oh, oh. That boat in the backyard? That's ours. I just picked it up the other day."

"For free you got that aquarium?"

"Well, not really *free* free. Cheap, though. Got a real good deal on it."

"What's a good deal on an aquarium?" she asked. "Right around four hundred dollars?"

"Yeah, I guess right around there. A little less, actually. I mean, that's practically giving something like that away."

Still Hilary wasn't warm. She pulled the afghan tighter around her neck, a noose crocheted in three acrylic shades of brown.

"I need that money," she said.

Her calm was making him nervous, she could see it in the way his toes curled up in his flip-flops. "I meant to tell you, babe," he said. "I was gonna surprise you."

"You were going to tell me, or you were going to surprise me?"

"Both, I guess. I'm gonna have the money back real soon, once that fer-de-lance has her babies. Then I'm gonna get a couple king cobras in there, babe, *king cobras*, and you know what those are gonna go for once I can sell king cobra babies?"

Hilary let out a breath she didn't realize she was even holding. The bile lodged at the base of her throat tasted like the Teenies her mom gave her as a kid, the red and blue and orange liquid in plastic barrels that passed for juice in families like hers.

"I thought you said those fer-de-lances didn't mate," she said.

"Not this time, maybe. But they will soon. It's their nature, babe. They got nothing else to do but eat and have intercourse, you know?"

Hilary shifted in her seat.

"Why did you take that money without asking me, Jack?" she asked.

"It's for both of us, anyway," he huffed. "It's an investment. Think about our future, babe."

"Why did you take the money?" she asked him.

"Listen, I should've said something beforehand. I don't know," he answered.

He didn't know, that was for damn sure. He didn't know a god-damned thing, not even enough to know that she was just about due for an apology that, even at his best, he probably wouldn't ever deliver. How could she have ever expected any different, when had she ever heard an *I'm sorry* out of him? From anyone, but especially from him. She hated him for that. She hated everything she ever loved about him in the first place. They were stupid, all those things. They were the Valentine's cards passed out in grade school. They were the messages on candy hearts. *I love you. Love me. Be mine.* Something airy and pretty spun out of sugar that dissolves into nothing once it hits lips.

"Those fer-de-lances aren't having any babies, I am," Hilary said.

"What?" Jack said.

"You went and got me pregnant."

"Ain't you on the pill?"

"I was until you smoked my pill money away."

"Well goddamn, I mean that's good news. We're going to have a baby, baby!" Jack laughing at his own dumb puns and her once upon a time finding it cute was reason enough for people like them not to be procreating, she figured, and him dropping down next to her and wrapping his arms around her tender-as-hell breasts was just the salt on top. But Hilary didn't move, not even to brush his wretched hands off her. She was unshakeable as the earth, or at least as unshakeable as the earth felt until it gave way under the unsuspecting feet of the entire populations of Turkey or San

Francisco. She felt that first tremor now, a little, tiny crumbling of some layer deep, deep inside her. But up top she was still steady, her voice not sounding off any alarm signal for the kind of violence building in her core.

She said, "We're not having any babies, Jack. We can't even keep a dog around here. Or at least one of us can't."

"That's not fair, Hilary. It wasn't my fault that door was broken. Besides, I mean, a dog ain't a baby. I'll keep an eye on a baby."

"Bring me that money or I will kill you."

Jack stood up and put his hands on his jutted hips, those gorgeous jutted hips she wished to God she'd never let rock over her own. "Heck no. This is our baby, Hilary. I ain't gonna bring you any money to kill our baby."

"I will kill you," she answered.

"Baby, it's just your pregnant hormones acting up right now. You're not thinking straight. Don't get crazy. This is our little Jack Jr. we're talking about, not some dumb mutt. We'll work something out."

"I'll work something out. Get out."

"No, I'm not getting out."

"Get out!" she yelled. "Get out now!"

Jack put his hands up like he was blocking the uppercut she'd only once tried to lay on him. "Fine, Hilary, I'll get out," he told her, "but I'm coming back when you cool down. Jeez Louise, Hilary."

Hilary didn't move from the afghan when the door shut over Jack's figure. All the pot had rendered him incapable of really fighting back like a decent man, and all his indifference had finally made Hilary not even care all that much about it. But now, suddenly, whatever it was that had burrowed itself into her womb set off like a tectonic plate the kind of deep-down meanness she normally let out just a little at a time. It was Jack's own fault. She never made like she wasn't mean at the core; it was an inheritance like her freckles and short legs. All she remembered of her daddy was the pistol he pulled last time he walked out and the blue-and-darker-blue puffer jacket that was left hanging in the hallway closet for years, oozing polyester stuffing like mildewed, endless guts. Only he also left behind a meanness heartier than the parvovirus that killed every housecat they tried to keep for ten years, a meanness that infected Hilary's mother and once-sweet-now-felonious little brother and Hilary herself when she let it. But she spent a long time being good and enjoying sunsets and loving Jack's flesh so hard that she figured she'd built up a pretty good dam between that anger and the world, with maybe just a few cracks and fissures in places that got patched up pretty quick. Now that baby they'd made was floating in the contaminated well in the pit of her belly, and no way in hell she was going to let something stew in that devil's water and then emerge into this world nine months later. Jack should've known better. He should've known all about poison, what with those venomous snakes that he spent all his time and all her money on. All that money that she earned, and meanwhile the thanks she got was a missing dog and rotten baby in its place. No, fuck him, she thought. Fuck the hell out of him.

Hilary ran the short hallway to the bedroom and flung open the door to the closet, where aquariums were stacked and shelved into something resembling the cheap apartment complexes where Hilary'd been raised and where Mexican blankets served as doors. She slowed when she approached a fer de lance, struck her finger against the aquarium where the snake lay wound into a loose coil. The snake's slitted tongue flicked but her eyes made no movement, no gesture of recognition or even acknowledgement of her presence. Such is a snake, Hilary thought. Such is a creature who responds to nothing but warm blood, be it enemy or prey. Every few weeks Jack would warm a rabbit carcass in a tub of hot water before he dropped it into the cage, the vague heat of the flesh the only stimuli the fer-de-lance needed to take the body entirely in its mouth in a flash so quick it never ceased to spook Hilary. The fer de lance worked on instinct entirely, would've gladly substituted Jack's flesh for the rabbit's had Jack ever given it the chance. "And then one, two—I'd be dead," Jack'd told her. The locals who lived in the fer de lance's native soils called it the Two-Step Snake because, he said, victims can only take two steps before crying uncle, dead or writhing on the floor dying.

This is what Jack chose to love, a serpent with one trick and that was killing. The fer-de-lance wasn't even all that pretty—little diamonds of earth tones flecked its skin, nothing so exotic as a green mamba, whose color hinted at the potency of its venom. This brown thing is what he had chosen. This, and whole bunch of other tubes just like it. She wondered if he could even name what he loved about her, his own wife, save for her tolerance of his snakes and bouts of stoned silence.

Hilary tapped the glass again. Nothing. Nothing out of any of the snakes in any of the cages, no sign as to whether they were even asleep or awake, if snakes even slept at all. She lifted the aluminum handling stick from the floor and rapped it against the cage, harder, stepping back the few feet the stick allowed her. Still nothing.

"Come on, wakey wakey," she whispered.

Hilary stepped as far back as she could and nudged the corner of the mesh screen that rested atop the cage. The fer de lance moved its head an inch over its coiled body and flicked its tongue again. Hilary's heart rattled against her breastplate and she stepped back further, hand on the door, until she practiced the breathing exercises she'd been taught at traffic school and worked up the nerve to step back inside. She was okay. She'd be okay. A jagged rock weighted the cover onto the cage, and as long as it stayed there, the snake couldn't go anywhere.

But that was the point. Hilary wanted the snake to go somewhere, wanted to carve a path for it to follow that led straight to Jack's heart, maybe dosing it with a venom so powerful that it would kick-start it just long enough to release the backlog of love Hilary hoped was in there before the necrotizing agent kicked in and rotted it forever. Hilary dropped a foot back until most of her weight rested outside the doorframe, so that only her head and arms leaned inside the closet, prodding and lifting the mesh. The fer de lance stayed wrapped around itself, its tongue flicking, smelling, detecting nothing more the cold aluminum of the stick. Hilary poked harder and lifted the lid higher and higher. She eyed the rock, the dead weight of it anchoring the lid onto the tank. The sweat of her palms left a ghost of her handprint on the stick, and she repositioned, gripped tighter, and finally swept the rock off the top of the cage. It landed on the floor with a thud that only scared her; the fer de lance lifted its head casually, as if it knew damn well who would win this duel. Hilary readied herself again, gripped the stick, and lifted the lid off the cage in one explosive twitch that landed the mesh on top of the rock. Hilary watched the fer de lance's head rise slowly toward the heat lamp before she backed out of the closet and slammed the door shut.

Hilary studied the space between the bottom of the door and the floor. About an inch—maybe not even enough space for the fer de lance to slither its thick rabbit-stuffed trunk through. It didn't matter, really. Jack would still get his when feeding time came again, thinking it was the warm rabbit the snake was waiting for instead of his own smooth flesh. But that wasn't quite what Hilary imagined. She wanted something with a meaning, a victim left forever alone on the bed he no longer shared with anyone but the serpent coiled on his chest. Or maybe his eyes open, one foot through the door, his collapse coming two steps into a run he'd hoped was his escape. She could see his shirt lifted up over his stomach, the jutted hip the last image of him she'd ever have, his normally white skin drained blue, and her right beside him, her own skin so translucent that you could see right through it, into her belly and the tiny, rotten pit that would make everyone understand why she'd had to do such a thing, that the ending of their lives was really the saving of them.

And goddammit, why did it have to be like that? She'd survived this long with blood so bad, maybe no venom could possibly poison it further. She remembered that night two months ago when Jack pulled her face to his as he came, and he left his mouth on her neck until his breathing slowed and his dick grew flaccid inside of her. She thought she'd been cured, she really had, as she laid awake for hours afterward so she could be conscious of this long moment, so incredibly rare was it that he keep her so close to him, as if maybe he'd had this course planned all along. Maybe Jack had really willed it there, this thing in her stomach, as if a child could be the antidote for the poison coursing through her veins. Maybe that's why she married him after all.

But who was she kidding, Jack didn't know any cure. He didn't even know the sickness. All this time she spent right in front of him, sleeping belly to belly, breathing in the air the other breathed out, and he didn't know a thing about it. They might as well have had an aquarium wall in between them all this time, so palpable was his shutter against her. And still all she wanted to do was believe in his hip the same way she'd done two years ago when she married him; hell, two weeks ago when she still hadn't been given a good enough reason not to believe in it. But now how could she go back? That hip was no cure, Jack himself was no cure, all he'd done was render her so complacent that she lost the will to hate him as much as he deserved, at least until he reminded her by burrowing into her own body, as if this would plant her here with him forever like a tree rooted in the shag carpet of their little, ugly rental home. And now this home that they shared was also the fer de lance's new native soil, and walking its ground would be treacherous. Hilary walked a trail back to the front door, balled herself onto the couch, and waited for Jack to come home.

How to Play Shit

My brothers, Kimi and Mike, left with their friend Carmen to steal some watermelon Now & Laters from the deli across the street from the one run by Joe. We didn't steal from Joe's because we knew him by name. Or anyways we called him Joe. We didn't know his name for sure. I don't know why we even called him that.

"Do you want to play Shit?" Carmen's sister asked me. I don't remember her name. From an ashtray she picked up a Virginia Slim that still had half an inch left to it and lit up.

"How do you play Shit?" I asked.

"You pull down your pants and shit," she said.

"I don't want to play that."

"Then how about Fuck?"

"How do you play Fuck?"

"You pull down your pants and fuck."

"I don't want to play that either," I said. Carmen's sister wore Lee Press-On Nails for Teens in Peachy Keen, and they poked into her cheeks and left crescent moons behind when she brought the stubby butt to her lips and sucked in. Or maybe the Lee Press-Ons just looked Peachy Keen because of the light coming through the brown curtains. The curtains were dung brown from the endless Virginia Slim smoke but they filtered the light pretty, so that every dirty thing in the room looked Peachy Keen.

"Baby," she said.

"You," I said. Carmen's sister wasn't a baby but she might have been a little retarded. She was fourteen but didn't go to school, not even Anderson, which was the school for retarded kids. I threw Blow-Pop sticks at the Anderson kids when they walked by, but only when their parents were with them, so they'd have someone to soothe their crying in case I didn't miss.

"Pull down your pants then," she said.

"Pull down *your* pants."

She did. "Your turn."

"You're weird," I told her. I wanted to go home—but not really, because their apartment was above a deli that sold Slush Puppies, and I liked being close to Slush Puppies even though you couldn't steal them because the machine was behind the counter. I didn't really want to stay and I didn't want to go, but that's just the way these things went. Everybody all around was always saying that sometimes in life you have to do things you don't want to do.

Domesticated Wild Things

Bobby and Danny were old enough to buy jugs of Blue Nun for underage girls, old enough to accidentally knock them up and have to set up house fast for themselves and their accidental babies, maybe even stick around for a few years if the underage girls stayed underage-enough looking after the babies were born and the WIC coupons started going faster than they ever thought they would. Instead they lived next door with their dad and grandma on the first floor of a triplex identical to the one I used to share with my daughter. Mirror image, I mean, as if the contractors had gotten a two-for-one on blueprints and drums of lead paint, then split for Daytona Beach before anyone thought to sue them if the kids turned out legally retarded. Those boys never opened the shades, but I knew it was their bedroom window across the driveway from mine—Aggie had started thrashing along to the Kiss *Alive!* forever streaming out of their room when she was still in the cradle, which made me think that if she hadn't died when she was five she might've grown into the kind of daughter I would've had to worry about. The kind that could've ended up on the poster I bet Bobby and Danny had on their wall, string-bikinied with bleached white hair and waxed white limbs that turned zombie-gray under stoners' black lights.

It didn't matter what was in their room, though, since they were almost always in the garage, a tin-roof box more like an abandoned horse barn than anything you'd expect to find in the industrial entrails of this town. I don't know why they bothered, really, because the car couldn't have been much safer in that box than it would've been out on the street. Anyway, why build a perfect replica of the General Lee, a '69 Charger complete with Confederate flag and a horn that blew Dixie, if you didn't want all the Yankees in Waterbury to stare?

Only I wasn't staring at the car on the walk out to mine, a Chevy Caprice that came off the production line primer-gray and stayed that way. Danny had the hood of the General Lee open, leaning deep into it, his ass as pale and broad as a surrender flag.

"Hey, Danny," I said, "mind sparing us this early in the morning?"

He straightened out quick and pulled up his trousers, spinning around so that his backside was no longer staring at me, even if his eyes wouldn't, either. It was then I felt a little bad: Danny was a quiet one, a fatty losing his pants on account of the fifty pounds or so that he'd dropped since the last time I'd really looked at him.

"My god, you're melting away," I said, thinking he might have taken it as a compliment, but he shuffled away to a toolbox and pretended to look for the socket for a wrench he wasn't even using.

"Son of a bitch looks sick, don't he?" Bobby said, even though Danny still had about forty pounds on Bobby, who had about six inches on Danny. Bobby sat on a dolly by the left front fender smoking a Pall Mall, canvas work shirt and thirdhand Lee's coated with oil, looking like a boyfriend in a Shangri-Las song. That kind of cigarette-and-accelerant combo was exactly what stuntmen used to set themselves on fire, I thought, only they did it for shit-tons of money and the kind of girls who posed in bikinis for posters. All Bobby had was a rumpled-up single sticking out of his pocket like a kerchief in an old man's suit, and me, a third-year student at a two-year college, and I wouldn't get into the backseat of the General Lee with him if the real Bo and Luke were back there to join us.

"He looks good," I said about Danny, but he did look a little bit sick. Still, I added, "It's you that's too skinny, anyway. It's the skinny ones that get taken down first in the animal world."

Bobby stubbed out his butt in a Savarin can full of grit. "That's right, you're training to be Doctor Doolittle down there at Mattatuck. In that case I got something to show you. C'mere."

Danny got up then and followed me and Bobby around to the back of the garage as if the command were meant for him, but when we got back there it was Danny who took the lead, crouching down over an aluminum take-out tray half full of kibble instead of pork-fried rice.

"There's this mother cat been hanging around back here. We been feeding her about a week now," he said.

"Nipples down to there. About a dozen nipples, man," Bobby said.

Danny's face turned as red as his ass was pale and pulled up his pants, even though this time I didn't point out that they were falling. "We been feeding her and stuff. Saw three kittens before, but now there's only two."

"Won't let us near them, though. The mother or the babies. Run into that brush if we get within five feet. They'll fucking eat our food, though. Got no problem doing that."

"They're tiny," Danny said.

"Typical woman, right? Let us pay for dinner but don't let us touch them."

"Other kitten must've died," Danny said. "Been trying to keep food out here for the other ones, but man, they're so tiny, I don't even know if that stuff is good for them or if it's too big for them to chew or what. Are kittens even born with teeth?" He looked at me like a child on Santa's lap, even though he still must've had a hundred pounds on me.

"Not full-grown teeth," I said. "But, I mean, if they're not weaned yet, as long as the mother's feeding on the food, she's passing it on to them through her milk."

Danny nodded. "Okay. Okay then. I'll just keep leaving the food out then. Maybe they'll come around to us."

"Lookit him, man, he's pussy-whipped," Bobby said. "Pussycat-whipped."

"It's dental hygiene now, though. I dropped out of the vet tech program," I said, because I had no idea if what I said about the cats was true, and because it would have been just dumb luck if it were, it was still some kind of lie by default, and that made me feel bad. Nobody laughed about it, though, even though it was a good opportunity to have one at my expense.

I couldn't blame Danny for getting so fat, when his grandma was always next door cooking up eggplant parm and a different kind of cacciatore for every day of the week. It was all bacon fat and red sauce over there, and sometimes the smells creeping into my kitchen from hers made the macaroni-and-government-cheese I made three times a week taste better and sometimes just bitter. And who knew where all their food came from, since grandma never left the house and Bobby and Danny's father only ever came home with twelve-packs of Meister Bräu, wearing what looked to be the effects of last night's twelve-pack of Meister Bräu. This kind of magic was why Italian sons never left their mothers, I guessed. Aggie had never complained about the macaroni and cheese I made her, though, or even the government-cheese sandwiches on untoasted white bread, so long as I used the star-shaped cookie cutter to turn them into something her little hands could hold, and it was only her grandma's gluey kugelis that sent her into a fit. I'd made her eat it, though, because we weren't the kind who could afford to throw away any kind of casserole. What I should've done was just tell her to eat around the overdone potato chunks and look for the good stuff, pick out all the bacon and put it alone on her plate, and I'd go ahead and feed off the rest of it. These things don't always come to you in time, I guess.

Danny, though, was taking all his calories for granted, still in the garage when I pulled in at a quarter past nine, way past dinnertime in the Pontevecchio house, orange work lamp hooked onto a rusted nail that looked ready to crumble into dust under the weight of the bulb and plastic cage. He sat in the passenger seat with the doors closed, radio tuned to WHCN and loud enough to bleed through the windows. His head didn't bob up when I pulled in or when I slammed the car door shut behind me, and I figured if he was staying out there all night to be alone, I wasn't going to be the one to ruin that by offering my company. But as I was about to leave, the window rolled down and Danny whispered, "Hey, Daina."

He didn't say anything to follow up, and he didn't need to, because I saw right away that what he wanted to show me were the two kittens curled up on his lap, both balled-up orange tabbies hardly bigger than tangerines, wedged in the crevice of his rack-of-lamb-sized thighs.

"How'd you get them in there?" I asked.

"They were just meowing out behind the garage, and the mother cat hasn't been around so they didn't put up a fight or anything."

"You should be careful. I mean, the mother might not take them back if she smells humans on them," I said, although I wanted to hold them too.

"Do cats do that too? I thought that was just hamsters."

"I told you it was dental hygiene now," I said. "Anyway, does Bobby know you have cats in that car? He won't even let your father in there."

"It's not just Bobby's car. I'm trying to keep them warm is all." He reached down and moved his forefinger over both of the kittens with more fine motor control than I ever thought a hand that size could have. One of them stirred and whimpered and let out a whine so faint and helpless that it must have been staged, and Danny looked up at me as if to say, *I told you so.*

I leaned up against my own car. "No, I mean, you're doing a good thing," I said. "It's just that you know they're not going to be safer in there if Bobby kills them for pissing on the seat. Can't you just take them inside or something?"

"No way, my grandma would bake them into pies. Can you bring them into yours?"

"I can't," I said, and I leaned into the window and ran my hand along their fur, so soft that I knew they wouldn't stand a chance against the elements, against any hard part of the many hard parts of the world out there. I spent a minute feeling bad, for the kittens and for Danny, but I didn't say aloud that the limits of my care had already been stretched, that the finite chunk I'd been given wasn't even enough to cover the one thing it was supposed to.

Then suddenly I realized how close to Danny's crotch my hand was and pulled it back. "I'm just never home," I said and turned away. "You should just take care of them. Not in here. You could build a little house for them out of boxes and keep them in the garage."

"The other neighbors might complain. George would find out," he said.

"George slaughters goats and chickens in his shed. He can't say anything," although George was the landlord and could say anything he wanted.

Danny looked down. "You got any spare blankets?" he asked.

"I don't got spare anything," I said. "How about one of your old flannel shirts? Those things can't even come close to fitting you anymore."

Just like that, Danny assumed the position he was in when I first pulled into the garage, chin tucked into his chest, hands folded like a praying man's and resting on his belly. He didn't ever answer me, and this time when I walked away, he didn't wave me back.

Thursdays were long days, seven thirty to five working the loading dock at Ferrule and six to nine thirty in class, so I came home to a dark house and kept it that way, feeling around for my own jug of Blue Nun and carrying it with me to bed, hoping that Sister might finally answer my prayers and coax me into the kind of dreams that wouldn't shake me awake three times a night. But just past eleven, I realized I was bored, hours away from sleep, wondering if I should've said yes to Rini and Leanne, who were always asking me to share whiskey sours with them at the Brass Pony after clocking out and who I was always telling to ask again when the semester was over, when I'd tell them no again for another reason. I could've turned on the old black and white for some company, but the rabbit ears on the TV were like the ones on the real bunnies after George took them in and then gunned them down in the backyard: useless. The speakers wired to my castaway stereo were just as shot, and anyway, the cassette deck still held the Barbie and the Rockers single that'd come with the doll I'd gotten for Aggie's fourth birthday. Instead I just tuned in to Bobby and Danny next door, who at that moment were going off the rails on a crazy train, if the soundtrack pumping through their window was telling any part of their story.

I kept the lights in my room off and stared past the curtains to the white blinds across the driveway. Backlit like that, Bobby and Danny were just silhouettes, shadows on a white screen like the world's crappiest burlesque. It was no problem telling Bobby's oblong head, topped like a Q-Tip with a puff of thin fuzz, from Danny's, which was heavy and full as a winter squash. Bobby walked in and out: taking a piss, I figured, and coming back to flip the record. Danny was out of sight for a while, lying on a twin bed that he'd outgrown before puberty, waiting for Bobby to step outside for a Pall Mall so he could switch the record or masturbate, maybe both if he could get it all done in six minutes.

But once both of them were accounted for, the door opened and a third figure appeared, and since it was at least three heads too tall to be grandma, it could only be Bobby and Danny's father. It figured that in this place, Ozzy would be something a family shared like a mug of wassail over the fire; for Aggie's sake I had to pretend to be as in love with Barbie and the Rockers as she was, but

Bobby and Danny were way too old for their father to have to do anything other than suffer their presence without asking for rent. But their father was really into the music from the way he swung his arms around just like Barbie of the Rockers when you twisted her at the waist: arms at forty-five degrees, one up while the other was down, something more like running in place than dancing or rocking, because not everyone knows how to follow a beat with their whole body.

And he was singing along too—I wouldn't have heard it unless he was really wailing, but his voice carried loud and long enough that he must've known every word, even if I couldn't make any of them out.

And then the record was over, but the singing wasn't, whatever it was that he chanted. And then the crashing of wood against wood, like a bureau knocked down and dragged across the floor to barricade against an armed robber, and I knew suddenly that it was too late: the bad guy was already inside, and the threat wasn't that his smoker's lungs couldn't carry a tune.

He yelled something that sounded like a cheerleader's rhyme: *Na na na Na na! Na na na Na na!* I couldn't make out the words, and Danny evidently didn't want to listen to them at all because he tried to drown them out with his own voice, the two of them together sounding like a shit symphony, worse than the one I played second flute in for three months in middle school. Then they were dancing just as bad, Danny's head to the left while his father's was on the right, then they switched sides, this three or four times, until Danny pushed his way through the doorway and thudded through what I knew from my own floor plan to be the kitchen. I skidded through mine, heard their door slam, and peered through the panes to watch Danny streak across the parking lot, wearing nothing but Fruit of the Looms that didn't cling to any part of his body, that instead filled with pockets of air like a parachute failing as he ran past the garage, up the hill to East Gate Cemetery.

I stepped onto the porch after Danny's father lunged off of theirs.

"Eat something, you shit!" he yelled. He slipped on an oil slick and fell to one knee, posed like a man with a diamond ring in his back pocket. "Eat the banana! Eat the banana!"

Danny didn't come back down the hill even after his father had quit chanting and gone back inside, leaving the mashed banana on the ground like a giant slug washed up after a heavy rain. It was a cold night, the kind of near freeze that starts in October and only ends when the deep freeze of real winter starts, and the air snuck right through the tight weave of my flannel pajamas. I crossed my arms tighter around myself when I thought of Danny up there in his whites, bracing against the wind in a corner of the mausoleum, hiding out until his father lulled himself to sleep with another twenty-four ounces of room-temperature lager.

"Sons of bitches are crazy, right?" I turned to the left and saw Bobby across the way on his own porch, smoking that cigarette I imagined him smoking twenty minutes before.

It wasn't the kind of question I had a response for, and probably not one he was looking for an answer to, so I just spun back around and said, "'Night."

The next morning the banana was gone, as if the thing had inched along as we slept and found its way from the blacktop back to the earth. In the garage, Danny was sleeping with the passenger seat of the General Lee reclined all the way down, somehow fully clothed, the kittens both balanced in a row on his belly like pom-poms on his navy Dickies jacket. He wasn't faking sleep, because people always get it all wrong when they fake it, posing the way we want whoever might be watching to see us, as easy to love as the kittens on Danny's gut. Real slumber looked like Danny's, as eerie as the stone bodies in Pompeii: mouths gaping as if there were something that needed to be said that couldn't get out. Limbs frozen at angles I never learned the names of in geometry.

A pile of fresh turd lay on the floor behind the driver's seat. It was cold enough for Danny's breath to pillow around him, but it was never cold enough for any pillow to smother a smell like the one that must've been in the car. I didn't want to wake Danny since he probably didn't get to sleep until after most of the neighbors had risen to make it to their four a.m. shifts and because I had exactly eight minutes to get to my job, which was ten minutes away. But better me than Bobby to find him like that, I figured, so I knocked on the window anyway. The kittens sprung to their feet and took cover under the driver's seat on the first rap, but Danny's eyes didn't shoot open until the fourth or fifth, and even then he took his time looking over at me, adjusting first to the light or just playing it cool, though I didn't figure on him having enough cool in the first place to do that.

Eventually he rolled down the window. "Huh," he said, matter-of-fact, as if I'd just fed him a piece of trivia that he already knew.

"Bobby's going to be out here any minute," I said.

"So?" he answered.

"So he might not be too happy about the backseat being turned into a litterbox."

Danny turned around to scope out the backseat himself, and when he finally spotted the pile he leaned forward in his seat and rubbed his temples. "Shit," he said.

"Yes it is." The kittens nosed around it as if it had been placed there by a force unknown. "I'm saying you should take care of it quick too."

Danny wasn't in a great big rush to do anything, it seemed, maybe waiting for grandma to bring him his morning coffee first. I didn't have any of that, but I did have a wad of Dunkin' Donuts napkins three inches thick in my glove box, so I reached into my car and grabbed them.

"Here Let's clean this mess up before you make me late for work," I said.

"I'm not making you late. You can go on ahead."

He was right, and since I didn't know what to say about that, I just opened the back door and scooped up the mess.

"I don't want to have to clean up after them," I said after I came back from tossing the wad into the metal trash bin outside.

"I told you you didn't have to do anything," Danny said.

"No, I mean, if I let them into my apartment. Until you find them a home."

"Oh," he said. He finally pulled the seat back upright. "Yeah, I mean, I'd come over to clean up after them and stuff."

"Better than you just did, I hope. You got two minutes to get some kind of box together for them. Shred up some newspaper or something if you don't have any kitty litter."

Finally Danny got out of the car and went to work. Because I didn't know why I was doing it, because I didn't even know if it was a favor, I was glad he didn't say thank you. I was glad he didn't say anything, not even good-bye, after we got the kittens settled in and I ran back to the garage and screeched the Caprice Classic out of its spot, the transmission never popping out of second when I sped away because I hadn't taken the time to warm it up.

It was funny how the kittens knew the shredded newspaper in the shoebox wasn't really kitty litter, but thought that the dirt in the one plant I ever managed to keep alive was close enough.

"Balls," I said out loud but to no one.

The little beasts came paddling out from underneath the sofa when they heard me cuss, right at home there in less than a day in a barely heated apartment. It was some kind of trick nature played, making baby anythings as cute as they were so that we'd never have the heart to drown them when they shat in the succulents we just transplanted.

"You guys hungry or what?" I asked them. They had to strain their necks so far up to see to me that I dropped down on my knees out of mercy. It was unfortunate that there was nobody there to rescue me, though, because once the first one clawed its way up to my lap I was a goner. I pulled their tails up to see what I was dealing with. A boy and a girl. They could grow up to be lovers, I thought, because the world of animals was like that, all kinds of messed up.

When a knock came at the door I knew without looking that it was Danny, so I yelled for him to come in. He carried with him a bag of kitty litter and a box of chow.

"Thank Christ," I said. "One of them went number two in my potted plant."

He shrugged, which wasn't really an apology, which wasn't really what that kind of announcement called for anyway. It wasn't until he kneeled down and picked up a kitten by the scruff of its neck, nuzzling it to his own, that I noticed the shiner on his eye.

"What happened to you?" I asked.

"Nothing," he said. "Bobby elbowed me in the face when we were working under the hood."

I didn't say anything.

"I'm serious. Hurt like hell."

"Accident?" I asked.

"Yeah it was an accident. You've been reading too many ladies' magazines. I could take anyone in that house out with one clock if I wanted to. I'm a grown man, for Crissakes."

"For a grown man, your father was yelling at you pretty good last night," I said.

"He was just getting on my case. Got nothing better to do."

"No?" I asked.

"It's just embarrassing," Danny said. "Letting the whole neighborhood hear."

"You get grounded?"

He didn't answer.

"How old are you, anyway?" I finally asked him.

"Twenty-four," he said.

"Goddamn. Seriously, Danny, maybe it's about time you start thinking about moving out."

"I'm working on it. You don't make that much stacking cans at PathMark."

"Especially not part-time. Especially when your car sees more of that money than your piggy bank ever does."

"You're not my mother. Don't worry about it."

"I can't be your mother. You're older than me," I said.

"You can't be my mother 'cause I already have one. Actually I been thinking about staying with her for a while."

The buzz of the ungrounded refrigerator was so loud that at first Danny didn't hear what I finally said, so I repeated it, even though by that time I had a chance to think about it a second time. "I thought she was dead."

"Huh?" he asked. "Why'd you think that?"

"I just never saw her around. I just . . . mothers are usually the ones who are around."

"She's in Naugatuck. Down by Hop Brook."

"Well," I said. "That's ten minutes away. With your mother. Not exactly what I was talking about when I said 'moving out.'"

He pulled himself back up to his feet, cinching his pants back at the waist even though they wouldn't stay there long. He was going to need suspenders soon to keep them from falling straight to the floor. "You got a couple bowls or something we can use for food and water?"

"The cabinet to the left of the sink," I said.

"Anyway, I'm trying. Not everybody can get their life together so easy like you."

"Oh, ha. Like mine. Ha," even though I realized quick that he didn't mean it as a punch line. "You think my shit is together?" I asked.

"Look at you," he said.

I looked at me. I looked at my legs twisted pretzel-style on the linoleum, the brown soles of my tube socks that only I knew didn't match. I looked above the fifthhand kitchen table at the oil painting of gourds out on loan from the library, at the string art of an owl with its right wing unraveling, at the three days of newspapers I subscribed to for the obituaries and the circulars only.

"Yeah," I said. I rubbed on a kitten's belly until it wrapped its limbs around my hand with a grip meant to kill. It bit into my palm and broke skin and licked the skin it broke. Then, when Danny poured some kibble into a bowl, the kitten leapt off and sauntered towards it, nosing its brother out of the way.

"What a hunter," I said. It was hard to say for sure whether the two were wild domesticated things or domesticated wild things.

"They're starving," he said.

"How about you, you're wasting away. You hungry? I got some mac and cheese in the fridge."

He shook his head. "Nah, nah." He got on all fours and put his face down to the bowl, not to take from it, but to offer it. "You're all taken care of now," he said to them, three or four times, as if he didn't know that he could repeat it forever and they'd never understand. Finally he looked at me. "I heard about your daughter. I'm sorry that happened."

"You should eat," I said.

"My dad tripped over a kerosene heater once and set the couch on fire. Got it under control in time but, shit, those things are dangerous. It could've spread real fast."

"Water? Anything? I can make hot chocolate. I got all this powdered milk."

"Them things should be illegal. Can blow up at any time."

"It wasn't a fire, it was the gas, the carbon monoxide. Coffee, anything?"

"I'm fine. I'm sorry. I'm alright."

The refrigerator clicked off, and it was quiet enough to hear the padding of the kittens' paws on the floor, limbs that seemed hollow they held so little weight, just enough to register, to remind you that they were real after all.

"Maybe I'll get to Goodwill and pick up a blanket for them to sleep on," Danny said.

"I have an extra one somewhere."

"Oh, really? You don't mind giving it to them?"

"It's not being used. Guess it's not really worth having a blanket that's not keeping anything warm."

"Thanks, Daina, that'd be really cool."

"It's in the closet in my bedroom. You know where it is," I said, because like it or not, we knew each other's homes outside and in. Everybody here knows how cold it can get.

Danny came every day around five thirty to feed the kittens and scoop the clumps out of the litterbox, which thankfully they started using after a few days. So when the six o'clock siren blew from Hamilton Park and still he hadn't knocked, and when the General Lee's horn started whistling Dixie nonstop a little while later, I knew I wouldn't be stepping outside to a block party.

It wasn't just me out there to see what was going on. George stood outside his shed, still gripping the backsaw he'd been using to build a hutch for whatever kind of creature he planned to raise into next season's dinner. Grandma stood on the porch, her limbs as thin as the veins in a maple leaf, and if the wind had blown strong enough in the right direction, it could've carried her over to the pile at the foot of Bobby and Danny's father. He stood just outside the garage, arms folded, tense and bobbing his head as if watching his boys wrestle Greco-Roman in states. Really they were going at it WWF-style, if the matches had been held in the inside of a classic Charger instead of a three-ringed pen: Danny just outside the driver's-side door, pinning Bobby against the steering wheel, mashing him against it when Bobby struggled.

"Get off me, you fat fuck," Bobby groaned, at least when he managed to get a breath. I could only make out the words when I'd gotten closer than their father bothered to.

"Are you going to do something?" I asked him.

He didn't look when he answered, "They're boys. Boys do it this way."

"Boys, right," I said.

The horn let out another verse of Dixie.

"Danny, come on, let go of him," I called, but instead he gripped a fistful of Bobby's curls, a gesture that almost looked tender.

"George is going to call the cops," I said, even though George hadn't said so or even moved since I'd stepped outside. But Danny let up enough then for Bobby to pull out from beneath his brother's hold, and he squeezed backward to the passenger seat and out through the passenger door. He stayed put once outside, shaking himself off, maybe just shaking.

"Motherfucker messed up. Keeping a dead cat in our fucking trunk," he said, only it didn't sound like he was talking to us or even to Danny. He was just saying it out loud, for the record.

When Danny answered, though, he looked straight at me. "I found it up at the cemetery."

"The shit was rotted, man. It was rotting in our trunk. No plastic bag, nothing."

"It must've got hit by a car or something. I was going to bury it when the ground was softer," Danny said.

"Yeah, hit by our car. Crazy bitch. That shit's been stinking our trunk up for a week. Motherfucker messed up," Bobby said.

"That's what he gets. His marbles are gone. He ain't eaten in a week," Bobby and Danny's father said.

Danny looked at my feet.

"Oh, Danny," I said.

Grandma began crying then and slammed the door on her way back inside, the snap of it a starting gun for Danny. "Fuck all this," Danny said, and he took off, almost graceful, running tippy-toe across the blacktop to my door.

"Goddamn, he's nuts. He's going into the wrong house," Bobby said.

I answered, "He knows where he's going."

I knew what he was in there for, but there was plenty else in that house going unused that he could take if he wanted. Wrapping paper saved from gifts I received to reuse on gifts I never gave. Three boxes of powdered milk on the floor of the pantry, donated by the state, given to remind women like me: your milk is as good as dust. Aggie's stuffed talking rabbit from two Easters ago, its batteries not yet dead despite the Peter Cottontail chatter that she'd played by pressing its palm a hundred times a day. Those are the things that are supposed to be temporary, the things you expect to give up. Danny was right after all: look at me. Look at all the shit I had together, things I could've been reaching out and grabbing for instead of drowning in. All the life rafts I could throw at him, with room for us both.

I looked to my left. Bobby and Danny's father was still shaking his head, a tic, some kind of palsy, or maybe he just hadn't cracked open his first can of steady. George asked, "What did you do with the cat?" and I hoped that he would offer to bury it, that it wasn't just triggering a taste bud. Bobby licked his finger and used the spit to patch together a hole in his Pall Mall, bent in the middle like a deformed spine.

"Jesus," I said. "No wonder. No wonder."

I watched Danny emerge minutes later with a box full of food and litter, both kittens dangling from his right hand by the scruffs of their necks. I didn't chase after him with the blanket, because more than likely he'd return home in an hour, maybe two, and he'd need something to explain why he came back, and I wouldn't need to hear it, at least not aloud.

IN THE PRAIRIE SCHOONER
BOOK PRIZE IN FICTION SERIES

Last Call: Stories
By K. L. Cook

Carrying the Torch: Stories
By Brock Clarke

Nocturnal America
By John Keeble

The Alice Stories
By Jesse Lee Kercheval

*Our Lady of the Artichokes and
Other Portuguese-American
Stories*
By Katherine Vaz

*Call Me Ahab:
A Short Story Collection*
By Anne Finger

Bliss and Other Short Stories
By Ted Gilley

*Destroy All Monsters,
and Other Stories*
By Greg Hrbek

Little Sinners, and Other Stories
By Karen Brown

*Domesticated Wild Things,
and Other Stories*
By Xhenet Aliu

To order or obtain more information on these or
other University of Nebraska Press titles, visit
www.nebraskapress.unl.edu.

CPSIA information can be obtained at www.ICGtesting.com
Printed in the USA
BVOW031341020713

324808BV00002B/2/P